Leprechauns & Larceny

A Paranormal Witch Cozy Witch Mystery

Book Store Cozy Mystery Series
Book 6

Lucinda Race

MC Two Press

Editor: Trish Long at Blossoming Pages Author Services

Cover design by Mariah Sinclair
Manufactured in the United States of America
First Edition February 2024

Print Edition ISBN 978-1-954520-73-8
E-book ISBN 978-1-954520-72-1

Pembroke Cove, ME

1. Robin's Cafe
2. Bygone Antiques
3. The Pembroke Cliffs
4. Cozy Nook Bookstore
5. Twisted Scissors Hair Salon
6. Betty's Market
7. Old Town Libary
8. Miss Judy's Dance Studio
9. The Sweet Spot Baker
10. Bee Bee's Boutique
11. Tuckers Hardware Store
12. The Copper Kettle
13. Police Station
14. Town Hall

Chapter 1
Lily

QUICK NOTE: If you enjoy Leprechauns & Larceny, be sure to check out my offer for a FREE novella at the end. With that, happy reading

I double-checked the time. It was just noon. I added the notebook to my tote bag. It had a never-ending list of to-do items for the upcoming wedding of my best friends, Nikki and Steve. As the maid of honor, I had taken on the bulk of the last-minute details while Nikki conjured up ideas for her wedding cake. As one of the best kitchen witches in our small town of Pembroke Cove, Maine, I knew it was going to be the most delicious cake ever, even if the theme was St. Patrick's Day and all things Irish. Not that I had a lot to compare it to since I had shied away from weddings. You know the saying, 'Always a bridesmaid, never a bride'? Well, I thought I was in that category until last fall when my forever crush and I finally made it official.

Detective Gage Erikson and I started dating, and even more recently, we got engaged.

"Milo," I called out to my gray tabby cat, who also happened to be my familiar. He was nowhere to be found. I wandered down the mystery aisle in my bookstore, hoping I'd find him snoozing in the soft kitty bed I had tucked into the corner for him. But it was empty.

"Milo?" He hadn't mentioned he was going out and I needed to get next door to the Pembroke Cove B & B to start decorating for the wedding reception. The flowers were going to be delivered tomorrow, so things needed to get organized. But not before I knew what had happened to Milo.

I stood in the middle of my bookstore with my hands on my hips and tilted my head back before saying in a loud and clear voice, "Milo, what kind of witch would I be if I left without talking to you?"

"Can't I get a catnap in without being interrupted?" His deep kitty grumble from behind me caught me off guard. I twirled around, thankful I was wearing jeans and not a long skirt which would have tripped me up, and I'd be on the floor with my familiar.

"There you are." I scooped him up and crushed him to my chest. "Where were you hiding?"

He tapped his paw, sans claws, to my cheek. "I'm not telling you since I'll never have a peaceful moment when the store is open if you know where to find me."

He rubbed his head under my chin so I knew he was just being cantankerous and not annoyed with me. We had come a long way in the last nine months or so when I discovered I was a witch after my family's book of magic, *Practical Beginnings*, had clonked me on the head.

Kissing the space between his ears, I set him in one of

the wingback chairs at the front of the store. "I need to run next door and see how the tables are set up for this weekend. Aunt Mimi was going to come down and watch the shop but had something else to do. Not that I know what's more important than this wedding."

"I assume Nikki is up to her wand in icing?" Milo stretched his body across the chair and got comfortable for his next nap.

I couldn't help but laugh. He knew her so well. "She's trying to come up with the perfect flavor combination that not only is fitting for a wedding but will also enhance the theme."

It was only recently that I had discovered wands and witches were a thing. Much to my delight, I had been to a charming shop in Boston called Wanderlings. It was there I selected my wand, and I took it with me everywhere. Even now, it was safely tucked into the bottom of my tote bag. Not that I was very good at using it yet, but I would be someday.

He rolled over onto his back and gave me a look. I knew what was coming next.

"I will scratch your tummy later. I'm already late." Slinging my tote bag over my shoulder, I gave him a quick pat. "I'll be back soon, so keep an eye on the shop."

"No worries, my dear witch. You can count on me." He yawned and I chuckled. "Maybe I should invest in security cameras to keep a watchful eye." I crossed to the door, and my hand was on the knob.

He opened his eyes and looked up again. "Now that's a great idea, or better yet, find the spell that will give you access to your store whenever you want."

"That's a thing?"

He sighed. "Tonight, try asking the book. You've made

great progress over the winter, but you might need to challenge yourself in the coming days."

That stopped me in my tracks. "Are you clairvoyant? Is there something specific I need to be ready for?" Since I discovered my powers, we'd had five murders in our sleepy little town and broken up a fraud scheme that had been brewing right under the police department's nose. My newly acquired skills had come into play along with my love of solving puzzles. Thank heavens, Gage discovered working with me only helped him solve the cases quicker than without me. In the process, a new witch and our friend, Dax Peters, had moved to town and joined the police force.

"Do you remember what Nikki mentioned at Halloween?"

Racking my brain, I couldn't bring anything to mind except that I had been focused on the haunted house the town put on as a fundraiser, the murder of Mathias Slone, solving said crime, and my almost demise. "You can't mean the casual mention of other kinds of paranormals coming to town."

"Anything is possible, and now you need to hurry. You said it yourself—there is much to do before the big day."

Instantly, kitty snores filled the room. I had to wonder, how did he fall asleep so fast and what did he know that he wasn't telling me? He hinted at information but never divulged the tidbits, letting me discover things as I got into a bit of trouble.

I opened the door and locked it, then added an extra protection charm around the building and Milo. He had become a part of my heart. Not that he wouldn't harass me about that later if he knew, but there was no way I could imagine life without him.

. . .

I hurried up the walk, and three men dressed like leprechauns grabbed my attention as I slowed my steps. I couldn't make out what they were saying, but their tones were laced with anger. They approached a dark SUV parked on the street. As the driver got in, he said, "I am not spending any more time waiting for John Bailey. We agreed, and—" The other two men got in, doors slammed, and tires chirped as they pulled away from the curb.

Pushing all thoughts of them aside, I entered Pembroke Cove Bed & Breakfast, and it was like stepping back in time to a home from a hundred or more years ago. A large fireplace dominated one wall of the spacious lobby. There was a small counter for guests to check in, and several tables to enjoy afternoon tea or morning coffee completed the space. Katherine Reese-White, the fourth generation of the Reese family to run the inn, was sitting on a small settee near the crackling fire. She looked up and smiled as I closed the oversized wooden door. She was ageless with her porcelain skin unlined, and her red hair cascading around her shoulders in a riot of curls. I knew she was older than me by at least ten years, but she didn't look it. What she did look like was an advertisement for an Irish lass.

"Lily, this is a surprise. I didn't expect you until later. In fact, I just got back from running errands, and I'm taking a few minutes to relax."

She started to get up, and I motioned for her to stay seated. "Katherine, relax. I came over to move a few tables around in the dining room. Nikki is working on her cake and asked me to fill in for her."

She pointed to the chair on the opposite side of her. "Join me for a cup of tea first and a cookie from the Sweet

5

Spot. It's your mother's special energy blend, and I couldn't resist stopping to see William this morning while I was out. He has the best selection of sweet treats every day."

At the mention of tea and cookies, I eagerly accepted. A cup was just what I needed to power through the rest of the day. And even though my mother wasn't a witch, she had a gift for blending teas that not only fixed what ailed me, but also tasted amazing.

She handed me a delicate china mug, and I placed a small sugar cookie on the saucer before I sipped the hot brew, knowing it would slide through my veins and give me a much needed boost.

As we enjoyed our tea and treat, I could tell the tea was working its magic. "This is just perfect. Thank you, Katherine." Sitting by the cozy fire and drinking tea was a rare treat. "Do you enjoy a cup every afternoon?"

"I try to in the winter with the days so long and dark. But along comes Saint Patrick's Day and the days are getting longer, and my days get busier, so there's less time to indulge." She smiled over the rim of her cup. "This weekend will be hectic with the out-of-town guests for Nikki and Steve's wedding, and we also have some folks in town for the annual parade."

Thinking of a parade with shamrocks and leprechauns wasn't my idea of fun. "How many people usually come up for the events? I thought Boston or even Portland would be better attended than our little town."

She waved her hand in a dismissive nature. "The group is always looking for buried gold. History states that a pirate ship crashed on the coast, and the Irish sea captain stashed his gold somewhere in Pembroke Cove. Now the new rumor is the only time it can be found is for three days—March sixteenth through the eighteenth. This year most of the treasure hunters are staying at the motel out on Highway One, but we have four regulars who always stay here. One man, John Bailey, is so enthralled with all things Irish that he stays dressed in costume for the entire event." She smiled. "It's quite a hoot, and, of course, it's good for business."

"That sounds interesting, but why dress up?"

Her eyes twinkled. "He says it helps him focus in his search for the leprechaun's treasure. I'm not sure if it does, but it's all in good fun."

I was anxious to get into the dining room and start the setup. "Are the reception preparations I'm doing today going to put a crimp in serving breakfast?"

"Not at all. I'm going to put a small buffet in the sunroom for tomorrow morning."

"Oh, good. Not that we can change the reception venue at this late date, but since you have guests who come year after year, I wouldn't want to leave a bad taste in anyone's mouth."

"It's a wedding and who doesn't love love?" She swirled her cup and turned the leaves out onto the saucer. "I missed the chance to have you read my tea leaves at the harvest festival. Any chance you'd like to take a peek now?"

The last thing I wanted to do was a reading since the last time I saw a man's bad fortune and he ended up dying. "I can, but I'm not very good at it."

She arched a brow. "That's not what I heard from a few people around town."

My stomach clenched. Did people know I had tried to warn Dean before he left the festival? I shook off the memory. "Think of what you'd like to know, and then we'll look."

"It's important for me to know if my business will continue to do well."

Katherine handed me her cup, I looked and was pleasantly surprised. At the top left of the cup was a cross. At the bottom right, it resembled a cow, and near the handle was a dagger. All in all, not bad.

She scooted forward on the settee. "What do you see?"

I pointed to what I interpreted as a cross. "Here looks to be a bit of trouble, but I wouldn't be too concerned." I pointed to the next area. "This symbol is a dagger which represents help from your friends and the cow in the lower right is a sign for good things to come."

She beamed. "I knew it. When I woke up this morning, I had a feeling that things were going to start going my way for a change."

I wanted to ask her additional questions since that was an odd statement, but I didn't want to pry, even if my curiosity was poking at me to ask. "Is business looking good for the season?"

Katherine knew I was referring to the tourists arriving around Memorial Day through Labor Day. Typically, it was absolutely crazy in town every Friday to Sunday. Once the calendar turned to July and August, the tourists multiplied exponentially. The weather for those two months was as close to perfect as one could enjoy in Maine.

Her smile stretched from ear to ear. "I'm booked solid. In addition to the usual guests, I've even booked two small weddings about the same size as Nikki's. Once she shared with me her ideas, I asked if she'd mind if I borrowed them to promote the inn. Being the sweet lady that she is, Nikki even offered to be the caterer and in-house wedding cake baker too. I think it made all the difference for my reservations."

"That's amazing." I wouldn't be surprised if Nikki had lent a special kind of magical touch to the wedding packages to help Katherine out. She had struggled with the workload the last couple of years since her husband, Donnie, started running treasure hunting charters. He'd be gone for several days at a time, cruising for treasure up and down the coast. He wasn't around much to help with the B & B. Hopefully, having more guests meant a higher cash flow and the ability to hire more help.

As if reading my thoughts, she said, "When I told Donnie the news, he agreed I could hire additional people to help out since he's gone so much during the season."

"Are you looking for more help? I'm sure we could post an ad on the community bulletin board at the town hall or maybe even reach out to the high school."

"Lily, what a good idea. I'll stop in at both places tomorrow. With a bit of Irish luck, I might be able to hire a few people and get them trained before the season gets busy. I knew sharing a cup of tea with you would lift my spirits." She got to her feet, "Now, let's go check out that dining room and start pulling it together for the reception."

I was feeling energetic and ready to pull out my wand, but I wasn't experienced enough yet to use it to create the perfect scene for a wedding reception—or much else for that matter. Right now, my spell casting was good with one spell at a time.

"Lead the way, Katherine." I slung my bag over my arm and touched the edge of my book, *Practical Beginnings*. I figured having it with me was a good idea since I never knew when I might need a new spell.

Chapter 2
Lily

I pulled out the checklist that Nikki had given me. First, I was going to make sure everything had been delivered and then start arranging the tables. Next, I'd set the tables with the china and gold flatware that Aunt Mimi had provided for the event.

Katherine unlocked and pushed open the double glass doors with enthusiasm. "Ta-da." The words faded away to a gasp.

Tables were overturned; plates and glasses were shattered. I expected to see a garment bag hanging on the rack just inside the door, but it was empty. When I looked down, I saw the veil had been tossed to the floor. My hand flew to my mouth as I stifled the first impolite word that popped into my head. Stepping over broken dishes, I moved deeper into the room. I couldn't believe what was right in front of me. Squeezing my eyes shut, I hoped when I looked again, it would just be a nightmare. Unfortunately, when I did, the destruction was still there.

Katherine's expression was one of horror. "Lily. I have no idea what happened. Nikki dropped her dress by earlier today, and I was going to put it in the bridal suite later. But I had guests checking in and errands to run so I had Nikki hang it up in here and decided when you came in, we'd go up together."

"Maybe you forgot you took it upstairs?" I knew my suggestion was weak, but I was grasping at straws. In my heart I knew that whatever mayhem had happened in here, the dress was gone. I had to call Nikki and break the news, but I also needed to call Gage. This was a crime scene, and it had to be investigated before anyone else came into the room and inadvertently trampled an important clue.

I glanced at Katherine. "Can you turn on all the overhead lights?"

She went to straighten a chair, but I put my hand out and stopped her. "Don't fix anything. The police will need to see the room as it is."

I made a slow walk around, taking it all in. Withdrawing my phone, I began taking pictures of the smallest detail. Once Gage arrived, I wouldn't have the opportunity, and this was a crime I was going to help solve, especially the missing wedding dress. If it was really gone, and by the looks of the veil askew on the floor, it confirmed my fear it was stolen.

K atherine had snapped on every light switch, and the room was now more like high noon on a summer day. A stack of emerald-green tablecloths was in a heap on the floor near the temporary bar. I crossed the room in a few steps, wondering if whoever had knocked them over left a clue. It was then I took a step back. There was no time to waste. A pair of leprechaun boots sticking out from under the linens changed everything.

. . .

Gage was not just a great detective on the Pembroke Cove police force but also my fiancé, and he answered the phone on the second ring. "Hello, sweetheart. This is a nice surprise."

The sound of his voice brought my heart rate down by at least twenty beats. "Hi. I'm at the B & B with Katherine. I was going to start setting up for the reception. You know Nikki is working on the cake, and I said I'd take care of this for her. Well she stopped over earlier today and dropped off her wedding dress, and then Aunt Mimi and Nate were here too—you know they were happy to let Nikki and Steve borrow the china and flatware." I knew I was rambling, but since Gage hadn't interrupted me, he knew this was not headed in a positive direction. "When Katherine let me in the dining room, we discovered the place was a mess, broken dishes and shards of glasses everywhere, and Nikki's wedding dress is missing. We're going to check upstairs just to be sure it's not in the bridal suite, but Gage, you need to get over here and fast. I saw a pair of black boots sporting large buckles." Finally, I inhaled a ragged breath.

"Are you safe?"

I liked that his first question was for my safety. He was so sweet. "I am and I'm with Katherine."

"Was the door locked when you went in?"

"It was."

"Alright, I want you to lock the door with you on the opposite side. Secure it with a spell just to be sure it will stay locked. I'll be there in a few minutes, and Lily, don't let anyone in the building, not even a guest until I get there."

"Okay. Don't worry. I think it's just me and Katherine here right now."

"I'm on my way."

Gage hung up, and I gestured for Katherine to move into the hallway. "We need to lock the door and wait for Gage. Oh, and he doesn't want anyone else coming in the building, so we should lock the front and back doors."

She nodded. It seemed shock had taken away her ability to form a sentence. I headed toward the kitchen where I knew there was a back entrance. "Katherine, what room were you going to use for the bridal suite?"

She held up one finger.

"Is it locked?"

Katherine shook her head.

I changed direction and moved toward the staircase. "I'm going to run upstairs and take a look around. You lock the front door and wait for the police."

She nodded. Hopefully, the shock wouldn't last long as there would be questions she'd need to answer when Gage and his team arrived.

I took the stairs two at a time and looked right and left. It seemed the numbers grew to the right so I headed down the narrow hall to the last door on the left. It was standing open. Cautiously, I stepped inside and crossed the bedroom to the dressing room. It connected the bedroom and luxury bath. I pulled open all four of the closet doors only to discover they were empty. No dress. The vibe of the room was oppressive and didn't match the room's floral décor.

I shook off a sinking feeling in the pit of my stomach. Hoping to discover the wedding dress hanging in the shower to avoid wrinkles, I moved closer to the claw-foot tub. The white eyelet lace curtain was drawn closed. I eased it back. Recoiling several steps, my breath shuddered as it escaped my lips.

Lying in the tub, with legs and arms twisted in an

unnatural position, was a man dressed as a leprechaun, but he wasn't wearing boots. I leaned a bit closer to see if I could tell who it was, but with a fake full red beard, wig, and hat perched low over his eyes, I could only see the tops of the man's cheekbones.

I backed out of the room and took note of the few items that I had touched since I needed to be fully transparent with Gage. I had unintentionally contaminated his crime scene. Before I left the room, I took a close-up picture of the victim's face. He looked as if he were sleeping, so it shouldn't be disturbing when I asked Katherine if she recognized him.

Once I reached the bottom of the stairs, I glanced around. Katherine was sitting in the chair near the fireplace with her legs tucked underneath her. She was clutching her teacup and just staring at the embers of the fire.

"Katherine?" Before I could show her the picture and ask who the man was, a sharp knock on the front door broke the silence. She didn't look up. I said, "I'll get it."

As I pulled the thick wooden door open, Gage, Dax Peters, Sharon Peabody, and Mac Sullivan were standing on the wide front porch. A police cruiser and Gage's sedan were parked next to the sidewalk.

Relief washed over Gage's face, and his gaze skimmed from my head to my toes. I guess he needed to reassure himself that I was really okay. I wanted to give him a hug, but he was working and as far as I was concerned, I too was on a new case.

"Come on in. I did as you asked and locked the door to the dining room but before you arrived, I went up to the bridal suite to see if by any chance Nikki's dress was there."

Gage's face looked grim. "I can tell by the tone of your voice you found something more."

I nodded. "I may have discovered who the boots in the dining room belong to." I glanced at Dax before I looked at the stairs. "There is a person dressed as a leprechaun in the bathtub."

Gage looked at Sharon and Mac. "Peabody, you and Mac take the dining room. And Lily can show you where the boots are." He turned his attention to the newest member of the Pembroke Cove Police Department. "Dax, you're with me."

"Room one. Go to the top of the stairs, take a left and the room is at the end of the hall. The door's open."

Gage cocked a brow. "It's not locked?"

"No. Katherine had said it was unlocked and for the record, there was no dress." My shoulders slumped. "I have to call Nikki."

He put a hand out and touched mine. "Give me an hour or so before you do. I want to process both rooms first. Telling her now won't bring the dress back unless it's still at the inn."

Gage was right. Reluctantly, I nodded. Peabody and Mac were walking in the direction of the dining room when I stopped Dax. Dropping my voice to barely a whisper, I asked, "Is there any way you can detect magic in a room after it's been used?"

"That's always a possibility. Why?"

"The room held a bad vibe, but it's not something I've learned how to do yet. So, if you could do your thing…" I left the rest of the sentence wide open. I had recently discovered that Dax Peters was a witch, and his coven was based in Louisiana. When he decided to move to our small town after his last case was wrapped up, we welcomed him into our community with open arms. And ever since he saved my life, he had become the brother I never had but always wanted.

His smile was reassuring. "I'll let you know what I find out."

Gage cleared his throat. "I don't want Lily directly involved in solving another murder. The last case we came close to—"

Interrupting Gage, I flung my arms around his waist and held him tight. "My spell casting is much stronger and besides, I have you, Dax, and the rest of our friends and family as backup." I kissed his cheek. "Now I need to go unlock the room for your officers."

Gage and Dax turned to the stairs, but Gage paused with his boot on the first step. He nodded in Katherine's direction. "She hasn't moved since we walked in. Go on up, and I'll join you in a few minutes."

Nodding, Dax marched up the stairs and disappeared from my sight. I hurried after Sharon and Mac and under my breath cast the spell to unlock the doors magically before I used the key Katherine had given me.

Despite the circumstances, excitement skittered inside of me. There was nothing like a mystery to quicken my blood and exercise my brain.

We walked through the doors, and Sharon gave a low whistle. "This is quite a mess. It's hard to believe there was supposed to be a wedding reception here on Saturday."

I gave her a sharp look. "There will be a celebration here if everyone we know has to pitch in to make it happen. Nikki and Steve shouldn't have to postpone their special day because someone decided to become destructo-Joe."

Mac gave me a sidelong glance. "Who's that?"

I shrugged and flashed a half-hearted smile. "I just made it up. You know a common name combined with an abbreviated version of destruction. It seemed to work in this instance." My gaze swept the overly bright dining room. "Where do we start?"

Sharon said, "Why don't you show me the leprechaun boots."

I had never mentioned to Gage exactly how they looked, but my guess, the large buckles and time of year had him put two and two together. "They're right over here, Sharon, and you know what they remind me of?" I was the only person who dared call Sharon by her first name, and for some reason she didn't seem to mind.

She said, "Do tell."

"Remember in *The Wizard of Oz* when the house lands on the wicked witch of the east? Well, it's not a house, just green linens, but you'll see the resemblance is uncanny."

We got closer to the back of the room, and I stepped around to the side. "Well, dang. I'd better call Gage." I looked at Sharon and Mac. "The boots are missing from a locked room."

Chapter 3

Gage

I squatted next to Katherine's chair. "You should call Donnie and ask him to come home. I know all of this has been quite a shock."

"When he left with his crew this morning, everything was fine." Her face was drawn, and she glanced my way before looking back at the fire. "I heard Lily talking. How can some man be dead upstairs? Everyone was supposed to be out for the day."

I handed her a cell phone from the side table. "Give Donnie a call, and I'll wait while you talk to him."

Nodding, she took the phone and dialed, and then the corners of her mouth drooped. "Voicemail."

I had been in this position before when someone was trying to reach a loved one. It was never easy to watch when their efforts weren't successful. "Try him again in a few minutes."

Mac hurried into the lounge. "Detective, you'd better come take a look." I gave him the stern arched brow stare. When he didn't move, I said to Katherine, "I'll have Lily come out and sit with you."

She gave me a dazed glance. "No need. I'm fine. Just… processing."

I patted her shoulder and followed Mac down the hall. When I walked in, my gut clenched. Stunned didn't begin to measure how I felt. Once Nikki and Steve saw this room, they'd be devastated. And where was her wedding dress?

Lily was checking her phone, and Peabody was using the police-issued camera to document the scene. I gave Peabody a curt nod. "What have you discovered so far?"

She handed me a pair of latex gloves and I pulled them on. "Not much but the boots Lily discovered earlier are gone." She pointed to the pile of green linens on the floor.

"They were there." Lily held up her phone for us to see. "Look."

I stepped closer to the screen, and my first reaction was to ask her why she took pictures before we got to the inn. But scrolling through the images on her cell phone, I could have kissed her. But that was something I'd do later. Right now, I had questions and who had the answers was anyone's guess.

"I thought you locked the room?" I glanced around and didn't see another exit right away, but this was a dining room, and by fire code there had to be two exits.

Regret filled her voice. "Gage, I'm sorry. I had no idea there was another way in."

I gave her a reassuring smile. "How could you." The last thing I wanted was for Lily to blame herself for anything happening. I walked around the back of the room to where there was a portable wooden screen. Folding it flat exposed another door. Pushing it open, I discovered it went into a hallway. It was dimly lit so I pulled out my trusty police-issued flashlight and clicked it on. The first thing I noticed were puddles of melting snow. I wasn't sure if they were coming or going, but when I followed them to the back door and opened it, the tracks were clear; someone had walked into the building. Based on the tread impression, they were work boots, and they went into the dining room. An educated guess was by the time they reached the room, the snow was almost off the boots, and when they made the return trip, they were clean.

"Gage?" Lily was standing in the doorway. "Okay to come out?"

I knelt down and peered at the trail closer. Without looking up, I said, "Ask Peabody to bring the camera. I want to get shots before our only evidence finishes melting."

She disappeared and moments later was back with the officer. I pointed to the glob of snow that had the best impression of the boot tread. "Make sure you get some good close-ups. Not that I think we'll get lucky and find this boot, but we just don't know."

"Sure thing, Detective." Peabody began to click from all different angles. Giving the tracks a wide berth, I stepped over and directed Lily back into the dining room.

"Did you see anything outside the door?" she asked.

"No, just the tracks coming and going on the same path."

"Like they walked in the footprints as they left?"

I nodded. "If I had to guess, they thought the hall prints would have melted by the time they were discovered, and walking in the same spots blurred the treads of the boots."

She pursed her lips and narrowed her eyes as she scanned the room. "I wonder."

Crossing the room, she picked up the hanger from the floor. There was a wisp of netting which I quickly realized was Nikki's wedding veil. It hit me—that was Nikki's, and Lily had mentioned the wedding dress was missing.

I began to look behind every box and stack of napkins in hopes the dress was just tossed behind something. But I didn't see it. When I looked at Lily, she was clutching the veil to her chest with her eyes closed. Her lips were moving, but I couldn't hear what she was saying. I was sure it was a spell, and knowing her, she was trying to locate the dress. When her eyes snapped open, she frowned.

"You know we're going to have to call Nikki and Steve and tell them."

I nodded and my insides were like lead. If this was my wedding to Lily, I would be shocked at the mess, but more so, I knew Nikki would be devasted to learn her wedding dress was missing. The question was, why would someone take it?

"Lily, was there something special about Nikki's dress that would cause someone to steal it?"

She withdrew her phone and tapped the screen. "It's beautiful but not overly expensive, nothing like a designer gown that would make a quick buck."

Handing me the phone when she got close enough, I studied the picture and noticed the embellishments down the front of the dress. "Are those diamonds?" I gave her a quick glance and then enlarged the picture to get a closer look.

"Crystals and there are gold sparkles, but they aren't real gold flakes; it's just costume enhancements. The normal kinds of things that are used in dress shops." She tipped her head. "But we do have a bunch of leprechauns roaming around. Maybe they mistook the shiny bits as real." She held up her hands in the stop motion. "Far-fetched yes, but I don't have another working theory."

Mac said, "Detective, I found a wallet." He withdrew a plastic Ziploc bag from his evidence kit, and after taking a few more pictures of the location, he picked it up. Unfolding it, he said, "There's a driver's license. John Bailey. Says he's from Boston."

Lily took a step closer and he held it up for her to look at but to her credit she didn't reach for it since she wasn't wearing gloves. Despite the grim situation, pride pricked my soul. She would have made a great cop; her instincts were flawless. I guess it didn't hurt in the last nine months we've had five major cases in town that she helped solve. This wasn't her first fishing trip.

"Gage, I'll bet he's with the group of treasure hunters from Boston who come up every year at St. Patrick's Day to search for the Black Sam Bellamy treasure."

I could feel my face go blank. What the heck was she talking about, pirate treasure?

"You know. We studied it for local history when we were in school. He was a pirate that plundered the waters up and down the East Coast in the early seventeen hundreds."

"What does this have to do with leprechauns in Pembroke Cove present day?"

Mac grinned and said, "You just asked the best historian and book lover in town for a lesson on the pirates."

I glanced his way and then at Lily.

Peabody, who'd come back in the room, said, "There's treasure in these here parts that I didn't know about?"

Her fake accent had me cringe. "Lily, tell us what you know. I'm not sure how it ties to the case, but right now, we have a dead body upstairs that we need to attend to."

"Right. Black Sam Bellamy was also known as the Robin Hood of the sea. He died in a wreck off the coast of Cape Cod, but that was obviously after he reportedly stashed chests of gold somewhere along the lower part of the

Maine coast. From what I've heard of the legend, it was enchanted by a leprechaun before it left port in Ireland. Now it can only be found by a leprechaun during the three days around St. Patrick's Day. Hence, we get an influx of grown men pretending to be leprechauns." She gave a satisfied smile and then it dimmed. "I wonder if that legend of the gold is why Donnie White became a treasure hunter. Maybe he's been looking for this gold too." She looked at the back of the room. "He'd know about the extra door."

"The story is interesting, but let's not get derailed from the facts. We have a dead person upstairs, identity to be determined, a missing wedding dress, and a trashed dining room. I don't see a connection to Black Sam's treasure."

Lily murmured under her breath, "Yet," and crossed the room, turned to look over her shoulder, and said, "Are you coming? We need to find out who the dead leprechaun in the bathroom of the bridal suite is and what murder weapon was used."

I followed her and said, "Sounds like a game of clue to me." Mac and Peabody grabbed their kits and hurried after us. One thing was for sure; this would be an interesting case.

There was a gurney and a couple of ambulance personnel standing to one side. They were waiting to move the victim. Dax was in the middle of the room with his small notebook in hand when we walked into the bedroom. He glanced up. "Find anything of interest?"

Lily said, "The leprechaun boots were taken. I didn't realize there was a door hidden behind a screen. And you?"

"I'm not sure what you sensed when you entered the room, but it was devoid of everything when I arrived. Your turn to share." His eyebrow quirked. She lifted a shoulder. "I secured the glass doors going into the room from the hallway."

He nodded, understanding that she must not have extended the spell to the room and just those two doors. I felt bad knowing she'd be hard on herself for not casting the spell wider, but we'd still find out who had come and gone with good police work. I leaned closer and whispered for her ears alone, "It's not your fault and I can tell by the way your brows are knitted together you're blaming yourself. Please don't. We'll catch the perp."

She nodded. "Nothing like a good puzzle to ease a tense situation."

I focused on Dax. "What have you found?"

Snapping his notebook closed, he said, "Nothing of interest. There is no apparent weapon, but I did discover blood on the tub, under his body. "Without plush carpets, there are no footprints to indicate how many people have come and gone since the room was cleaned."

Nodding, I knew what he meant.

Lily slipped her hands into her jacket pockets. "How does carpet help?"

Dax said, "With very dense carpet, if matted down when people walked on it, potentially we might have an indication of foot traffic, but it's a long shot."

"There had to be two people in the bathroom, and we can surmise it was an argument since after our leprechaun hit his head, someone closed the curtain to make it appear as if all was well, leaving the room with the door open as Lily found it."

I took in the room. It was pristine. "We'll need to dust for prints, but I'm sure you're correct."

Lily was near the small sitting area. She knelt down and

said, "Sharon, can you take a picture of this?"

"What did you find?" I asked, crossing the room.

She pointed to a small shiny bead and a flake of gold. "The wedding dress was in this room."

Peabody snapped several pictures and handed me another evidence bag. "I'm going to check the area for any more sparkles. Mac can handle the bathroom."

I extended my hand to Lily as she stood. Giving mine a quick squeeze, she let go, her face grim. "I don't understand what anyone would want with that dress."

"Lily, I'll check all the closets again to see if there is any indication the dress might have been here."

"Thank you, Sharon." She gave me a sharp look. "Let's go see the victim. And I really need to call Nikki and let her know about"—she sighed and it seemed to come from the tips of her toes—"everything."

As we entered the oversized bathroom, the first thing I noticed were the feet hanging over the tub, wearing the brightest emerald-green socks I'd ever seen and stitched on the heels were pots of gold. Going closer, I saw the victim was dressed in matching green pants and a jacket. A thick red beard covered his jawline and mouth. As Lily had described, his hat was pulled low over his head, obscuring his forehead and eyes. All that was visible were his nose and cheekbones. His arms had dropped to the sides at an awkward angle, but in his right hand there appeared to be a paper.

Dax was watching me. "I saw it too but waited until after the scene was documented before I was going to look." He moved around to my right and eased in behind the claw-foot tub and wall. "You can see here the blood. An educated guess—he fell back, hit his head, and died here."

"Mac, do your thing, and then we can have the EMTs

come in and lift him out."

I moved out of the room and gestured with my hand for Lily to follow me. Peabody was doing a thorough search of the drawers in the dressing area and still seemed to be coming up empty.

I guided Lily to the opposite side of the room near the windows overlooking the back patio. "What are you thinking?"

"That I don't want to call my best friend and tell her what happened. She's in her kitchen creating her wedding cake, and we have no dress, a disaster of a venue, and well" —she jabbed a finger in the direction of the bathroom—"and him."

Mac came out of the room and said, "Detective, we're ready to move him."

"Lily, maybe you should wait here. There's not going to be a lot of room in there." I nodded to the EMTs and entered the bathroom ahead of them. I went to the far-right side so that I could have a good view of when they picked up our mystery man. With a bit of luck, another clue would be under him.

The gurney was positioned as close as they could get to the tub. After a short discussion on the best way to move him, they each leaned over and lifted him on the count of three. Once he was on the gurney, Mac stepped up and took another couple of pictures of his right hand before easing the slip of paper out. He took another picture of it folded and handed it to me.

The EMTs rolled the gurney out of the bathroom and Lily came in. She looked over my arm as I unfolded the note. Three words were scrawled in pencil.

I FOUND IT!

Lily snapped a couple of pictures with her cell phone. "Do you think he wrote it or it was given to him?"

"No idea, but this is police evidence and speculation won't help us."

"Gage, need I remind you that you wouldn't have even known there was a crime if it wasn't for me."

My temper began to perk a bit. "Need I remind you that—" Before I could finish, Dax interrupted me.

"Found it."

I cringed as it sounded just like the note our victim was clutching. From between the wall and the tub, he was pulling out what looked like a cream-colored dress.

Lily gasped. "Is that Nikki's wedding gown?"

He held it up by the neckline and it did look like a wedding dress, although now it was dusty and there were a few tears on the front where it had gotten caught on something.

She reached out to take it and I put a hand between her and the dress. "We need to process it for evidence first."

I had never seen Lily glare at me like she was now. "Lily, we have a dead man and a missing wedding dress. I need to follow protocol, even if this belongs to your best friend."

An EMT stepped into the room. I needed to learn the names of the new people on the squad. "Detective, did you want to have a look before we take the victim to the morgue?"

I gave a curt nod, and we all went out into the next room. Drawing the blanket down that covered his face, I tugged on his beard, and it moved easily as it was attached with an elastic band. Mac manipulated the wallet so it was open inside the evidence bag. I compared the picture on the license to the face looking back at me. "It's John Bailey."

Chapter 4
Lily

Annoyance roiled inside of me, but I held my frustration in check. "Gage, I need to call Nikki and let her know what happened. Her dress is in an evidence bag; the room where her reception is to be held is in shambles, and the wedding is in two days." I threw my hands up in the air and pointed to the EMTs pushing the gurney out the door. "And Mr. Bailey has left the building so unless you have any logical reason why she can't be told, I'm calling her." I was glaring at him, but I didn't care.

Sharon and Mac slipped out of the suite with Dax behind them. Gage said, "We'll do a final sweep of the dining room and then interview Mrs. White."

I smacked the palm of my hand to my forehead. "We, or I should say I, forgot about Katherine." I glanced at my watch and noticed it had been almost an hour since Gage and everyone had arrived.

Sharon paused in the doorway. "I'll check on her while you make your call."

I gave her a smile of thanks before she left. Why did we smile at each other during this awkward situation, when someone had lost their life in the next room? I reminded myself Mr. Bailey had the best cops on the case, and the responsible person would be arrested very soon.

Gage cupped my elbow in his hand. "Come on. Let's go downstairs and you can call Nikki, but give me a few minutes to contact Steve. I think he should be here when she arrives or even go pick her up."

Nodding, I said, "You go ahead. I'll be right down. I'd like a little privacy when I call her."

He opened his mouth, and I gently placed my hand over it. "I won't touch a thing."

"I know; it's just a force of habit." He pecked my cheek, and my annoyance evaporated. He was doing his job and once he left the room, I'd do mine. I needed to take a bunch of pictures for my clue board if I had any hope of following the evidence we had discovered. Too bad I hadn't done the same in the dining room before everyone arrived. Other than the boots, I had only taken a couple of pictures. But on the upside, I'd have a few minutes before Nikki arrived and maybe I could slip into the room and get what I needed.

I turned on the video camera and did a slow three-sixty, filming first, then I zeroed in on where I had found the embellishments from the dress before moving into the dressing room and then bathroom, repeating the process for pictures. Once I was satisfied I had captured all the details, I crossed the room to the wide windowsill and perched on it, then tapped the keys on my phone.

When Nikki said hello, I could hear the happiness in her voice. I hated to be the one to burst her bubble, but better me than Gage.

"Hey, Nikki. I'm over at the B & B." I had to launch into the conversation. It was like ripping off a Band-Aid—best to do it fast and deal with the sting after. "And there's been some trouble. You and Steve should come down." I took a deep breath. "And don't worry, we can set everything right for the reception."

"Lily?" I could hear the happiness bubble deflate as she drawled out my name. "What's wrong?"

Leading with the easy stuff first was the best idea I had. "Someone got into the dining room and broke a bunch of dishes and glasses, basically tossing the room like they were searching for something."

I heard a whoosh of air as she exhaled. "That's awful, but plates can be replaced and we can get that cleaned up."

"We can."

She paused. "What aren't you telling me? Hold on, Steve is ringing in." I could picture her looking at the screen.

I looked out the window and there was a dark lump partially hidden near the garbage dumpster. Gage must not have looked around when he was out back.

"I'm here. That was Steve and he's on his way to pick me up, and we'll be there in five minutes, but getting back to what you're not telling me, I need to be prepared."

There was no easy way to break the news about her dress and its potential connection to the murder. "There was a dead man in the tub of the bridal suite, and your wedding dress has been taken into evidence. It was found stuffed in the crack between the tub and the wall."

She laughed with a nervous undertone. "No, it's not. My dress is hanging in the dining room. Katherine is taking it upstairs after she gets back from her errands. She told me it was perfectly safe to leave it in there since she'd lock it up."

"I'm sorry, Nikki. I don't know how or why it was upstairs, but I promise you we'll figure all of this out."

With a strained sob, she said, "I gotta go. Steve will be here in a minute." The line went dead. I empathized with her reaction; she was in shock. I took a couple of pictures of the dark lump and hurried downstairs to let Gage know what I saw.

I didn't bother to go to the dining room but veered off into the small lounge where I assumed Katherine would be. When I rounded the corner, she was motionless, in the same chair, holding her teacup in her hand, staring into the fire. Gage was sitting next to her. He looked up when he saw me and I waved him over.

He cast a glance in her direction and crossed the space in a few strides. "What's up?"

"Did you look near the dumpster when you were outside?" I pulled up my phone and showed him the last picture I had taken.

"Dax!" he shouted.

He rushed into the room. "What's going on?"

Gage turned my cell phone around. "Can you and Peabody go out and see what this is and check for tracks anywhere else on the property."

"Sure." He gave me a wink and I knew he couldn't share what he found so I slipped him my phone and he nodded. He might be a cop, but he understood my need for clues and he'd take a few pictures. My place was in the building when Nikki and Steve arrived.

Katherine looked over her shoulder, her voice soft as she said, "Don't forget to unlock the front door. I'm still trying to reach Donnie. He should be down at the marina working on his boat, but he's not answering my texts or calls."

I said, "I'll take care of the door if you want to call

Donnie again, or maybe Gage can ask a police officer to go down and check on him?"

She shook her head, her face pale. "No, that would only worry him. I'm sure he'll call me when he can."

"Is there a landline at the marina where Donnie keeps the boat?"

"No. He must have his phone on silent. I could call Keith, Jock, or even Hutch. They work for Donnie and are probably with him since they were all here earlier."

"What time did they leave the inn?"

Katherine stared off into space. "It was almost ten, I think. Sometimes they meet Donnie here when they're going to work on the boat. You know in the winter. And today, when I came in from my errands, the crew and the men from Boston were all chatting about a charter on *Donnie's Treasure* for June. Well, all except for John Bailey. He hadn't come down yet."

"Was anyone upset?" Gage didn't react to the news that friends of our victim had been chatting it up with locals.

"Nope." She shook her head. "Oftentimes people will book charters when they meet Donnie's guys. I've gotten the impression it makes everyone more comfortable going on the boat with a crew they had met."

Growing up close to the ocean and knowing most of the captains and crews, I never gave it much thought about putting your life in the hands of people you didn't know, but it made sense.

Gage ran a hand through his light-brown hair before sitting down in the same chair I had vacated just a short time ago. His long legs stretched out in front of him, not because he was relaxed but the antique chair was lower to the ground, and he needed space for his legs. I smothered a smile but not before I saw a sparkle in his hazel eyes. He thought it was ironic trying to get comfortable in the smallest chair in the room, but he wanted to be close to Katherine. His voice would be laced with compassion while he asked her questions that needed to be answered. With any luck, he'd wait until after I joined them so I could listen.

"They're here." I hurried to the front door, not needing to explain to Gage how I knew. Nikki and I had always been like twins from other mothers.

I pulled the heavy wood door open just as Nikki reached the top porch step. She was clutching Steve's hand, and their faces were grim. I opened my arms and wrapped them around the couple. In this moment, it was all I could do. We stood like that for what seemed like an eternity until Nikki patted my back.

"Gage filled Steve in on everything. Before we see the damage to the room, can I talk with Katherine? I'd like to understand how this happened since it seems she forgot to lock up." She spoke softly but with an unmistakable edge of determination.

We stepped inside out of the blustery wind that had kicked up. "She's in the lounge with Gage."

Steve asked, "Who else is here?"

"Dax, Sharon, and Mac are in the dining room and outside gathering information." He gave me a sharp look but didn't say what was on his mind.

Nikki paused in the hallway. "Do you feel that?"

I stood still, not sure what I should be noticing. "No. What am I missing?"

"Residual magic."

Putting my hand up like a kid in school who really didn't want to answer a question, I said, "That was me. I sealed the doors after Katherine and I discovered the room had been ransacked."

Her face fell. "I was hoping a witch was involved. It would be easier to discover who it was since we all have our own distinct signature."

Now she had captured my interest, but this wasn't the time to dive into the new tidbit. I filed it away to ask her once things were somewhat normal. "I need to fill Aunt Mimi in on her dishes being smashed and the flatware missing. I know she'll be disappointed, but maybe there's a way she can fix them. I figure if anyone has a spell to repair broken china, it will be her." I held my aunt Mimi in the highest regard even before she became my witch mentor.

Nikki and Steve hurried down the hall. If it had been me, I wouldn't have taken my time either. When we entered the room, Katherine stood up and held out her hands to Nikki.

"I'm so sorry for what's happened, but I promise Donnie and I will pay for the damages and replace your gown."

Nikki glanced over her shoulder and mouthed, *Replace?*

Gage unfolded himself from the chair and shook Steve's hand. "Nikki, your dress had to be taken into evidence and typically, we don't return items to their rightful owners quickly. But I'll see what I can do to expedite things." He didn't mention that it was also damaged; that could wait.

"Thanks, Gage." Nikki focused her attention on Katherine, their hands still clasped. "Tell me what happened after I left. I thought you said all your guests were out for the day and you were going to lock the dining room. What changed?"

I considered Nikki's approach and knowing me, I wouldn't have been this calm. This seemed to be a better way; Katherine was less rattled and could fill in the blanks.

Nikki eased her back into the chair and perched on the

settee near her. Steve took the seat beside her and leaned forward. Gage had his notebook out, and of course, I was ready, and I was going to do one better and record it all. This was so the nuances wouldn't be lost when I was scrolling through my notes later. But I remembered Dax had my phone. Nikki's was visible in her jacket pocket. I slipped it out and engaged the voice recorder.

Katherine said, "Let's see. You left around eight thirty, and I locked the glass doors just like I said I would. That was after I had a couple of guests check in. You know they're here for the St. Patrick's Day events. All those people interested in hunting for treasure and eating corned beef and cabbage at The Clam Shack. Not that a seafood restaurant can do justice with corned beef, but Fred Wickshire does his best."

"Katherine, what happened after you finished checking in the guests, and do you remember who they were?" Gage stopped writing as he attempted to get her back on track.

"Yes, Dylan O'Hara and Arthur Nolan. They're friends with John Bailey, another one of our regular guests."

Gage's expression never changed at the mention of Bailey, but I knew my face had dropped. "Was there anyone else who came with them every year?"

"Yes, Shay Keegan checked in yesterday with John. I'm sure the four of them are poking around town somewhere dressed in their emerald-green wool coats and hats, wearing those ridiculous red beards in search of the supposed gold." She shook her head and a small smile graced her lips. "The only gold they'll ever find are the gold buttons on their jackets. But getting back to earlier, after I had showed my guests to their rooms and let them know where I would be serving breakfast for the weekend, we went our separate ways. I walked over to Tucker's Hardware for light bulbs. Then I stopped at the Old Town Library to pick up a couple of books I had on hold, oh, and next was the Sweet Spot to pick up a box of pastries and sweet rolls for breakfast tomorrow and then came back. I couldn't have been gone more than two hours. It was nice to get out and see a few people in town."

"Just so that I'm clear, you locked the dining room, checked in the guests, and when did everyone talk with Donnie and his guys about a charter?"

She tapped her chin and looked at the ceiling. "Huh, right before I left, I popped into the kitchen to check on the coffee supply. When I came out, they were talking. We went our separate ways, and then I ran my errands."

I skipped over the fact that she had repeated herself and asked, "Did you notice anything was amiss when you returned? Was the front door locked?"

Katherine tipped her head to the side. "The guests all have a master key to get in the front door and I used my key to get in."

Gage was quick to interject. "A master key? Will it get them into the dining room and other guest rooms too?"

"Of course not. Each room key only has two copies. I have one and the front door key is on their room key ring. As far as the dining room is concerned, there is only one copy for that, and I keep it behind the desk." The color drained from her face. "Which anyone could have used while I was out."

As far as I was concerned, that answered one burning question. "Did anyone see you lock the room and put the key back?"

She shook her head. "The room was locked before I did the check-ins, but for anyone who has stayed here before, I'm sure they'd know my routine and where I keep the keys.

But not the guest room keys. Those are kept in a lockbox under the counter."

Nikki took her hand. "So, you left the inn for two hours which means it could be anyone who vandalized the dining room, took my dress, and killed a man?"

Katherine's eyes bugged open. "Yes. It's not like I planned for this to happen." She looked from Nikki to me. "Lily, tell her the doors were locked when we went into the dining room."

I nodded. "They were but there was another door hidden by a screen at the back of the room that Gage discovered. It leads to a hallway and an exterior door that was unlocked. Anyone could have come and gone without being seen. And at this point, we have no solid clues to know who it was."

Chapter 5
Lily

Nikki got to her feet. "Lily, I have to see the room. Now."

Steve took her hand, and I loved seeing the bond my best friends shared. I glanced at Gage who was looking at me, his hazel eyes tinged with regret, and I got it. We were about to pour salt into a wound for Nikki and Steve.

I slipped my arm through the crook of hers, grateful we were only going to look in the dining room and not upstairs. With some luck, Katherine would have another room where Nikki could get ready for the wedding. "Now, everything can be cleaned and fixed. So, please, look at it through that lens."

She nodded and straightened her shoulders. "I'm ready."

We made our way down the hall, Nikki sandwiched between me and Steve. Gage was right behind us, and Katherine was a few steps behind him. We made quite a sorry-looking group, as if we were headed to the dentist's office for a visit without Novocain. We paused at the doorway and Sharon opened the door from the inside, effectively blocking the view.

"Nikki, it's not as bad as it looks." She stepped to one side and Nikki sucked in a ragged breath. Looking at it through her eyes, I was shocked all over again. The bright overhead lights didn't mask the disaster. Tables were on their sides; shards of broken glasses and plates were in small piles near overturned chairs. But this was nothing that a couple of well-cast spells couldn't clean up.

Stepping deeper into the room, she looked at the hook where I knew her dress had hung a few hours before. With a catch in her voice, she said, "What am I going to do about a dress?"

I squeezed her arm against my body. "As soon as we're through here, we'll go back to the bookstore. I'll get in touch with my aunt, and you can call your mom. We'll all meet at the shop and once we put our heads together, we'll come up with a plan."

I caught Gage looking at me, and he nodded in agreement. We needed to make plans for a different dress.

Steve kissed Nikki's temple. "Sweetheart, this isn't nearly as bad as I thought, and we will make it perfect again."

Katherine rushed forward, pushing her body between me and Nikki. "I'm not sure what to do about the dishes, but we can find a suitable replacement."

"Aunt Mimi has plenty more. It's like she's a warehouse for fancy china." I crossed my fingers behind my back since I knew she'd just fix what was here and make it look like there was more from an overfull attic.

I watched Nikki transform before my eyes, from a heartbroken bride to a powerhouse decision-maker.

"All right then, here's what we'll do. Once Gage has

released the room, which will hopefully be by tomorrow morning, we'll get it cleaned up and reset." She looked at Katherine and cocked a brow. "I'm sure you'll understand when I say I'm going to take charge of securing the room until after the wedding."

Katherine's gaze dropped to the floor. "Whatever you need, Nikki, it's yours."

"Will there be a room where I can get ready?"

Chewing the corner of her lip, she said, "It won't be as large as the suite, but I'll have it ready for you by tomorrow morning."

"Good and I'll take care of locking that room as well." Nikki plucked the veil from the hook and kissed Steve. "Honey, will you stop at Robin's Café and check with Regan? Ask her what time she plans on setting up the buffet warmers and platters tomorrow. I want to be here when she does."

"No problem. But I can take that off your to-do list if you need to finish the cake."

She narrowed her eyes as she glared at Katherine who was doing her best to avoid all eye contact with any of us. "I'll need to come over since I'm going to lock up *the room*," and she stressed, *the room,* to indicate it was more than just an ordinary key.

"Got it." He placed his hands on her shoulders and pecked her lips. "I'll see you tonight, and I'll grab dinner on the way home."

"Um," I said, "if it's okay with you guys, I was going to suggest we meet at my house and talk about today."

Nikki smiled. "That's code for we're going to tackle the new puzzle Lily has decided to help Gage solve."

I lifted one shoulder in a shrug. "I hope it's not in bad

taste, but maybe we'll get lucky and wrap this up before you walk down a flower-strewn aisle."

Steve said, "Just text me. I'll pick up dinner on the way."

I looked at Gage, Dax, Peabody, and Mac. "Everyone is welcome since I might as well put my cards on the table. I plan on helping you solve this case."

With a snort, Gage said, "I knew that was coming. Why don't we meet at Lily's around six?"

The group agreed, and Katherine piped up. "For what it's worth, I'm really sorry this happened, and there won't be any charge to use the B & B for the ceremony or reception."

Ever gracious, Nikki placed a hand on the older woman's shoulder. "Katherine, we know this isn't your fault, and you are as much a victim as I am in this mess. Not to mention the poor person who met an untimely death."

Katherine shuddered when Nikki very delicately mentioned John Bailey. "Steve and I will be paying you the agreed upon rate and we won't take no for an answer."

It was easy for Nikki to be forgiving; it was just the kind of woman she was. Katherine gave Nikki and then Steve a fast and bone-crunching hug. "If this had to happen, I'm glad it was you." Her cheeks went pink. Sputtering, she said, "Not that I wanted anything to mar your perfect day, but ... well..."

Nikki patted her shoulder. "I understand."

Waving Steve out the door, she said, "I'll see you later, and if you're looking for me, I'll either be at the bookstore or home."

He rocked from one foot to the other as he hesitated, as if he wasn't sure Nikki was as grounded as she seemed.

I steered him to the door. "Steve, don't worry. I won't leave her side for the rest of the day."

He said, "You're a good friend, Lily."

With the veil folded over her arm, Nikki said, "I'm going to call Mom from the lounge and ask her to meet us at the bookshop. Give me five minutes?"

"Sure." I waited until she left the room, and Katherine trailed after her. This day seemed like it was lasting forever.

"Any dinner requests?" I looked at my friends and Gage.

"Pizza is fine. Make it easy on yourself since the next few days will be busy," Gage said.

Sharon said, "After dinner, if it's okay with Katherine, we could all come back and clean up. That is if we're done processing the room."

What would take non-magical people a few hours to do would take my aunt mere minutes. Since Sharon didn't know anything about the witches of Pembroke Cove, I looked to Gage for help.

"Thanks, but it won't take much time. I'll need you and Mac to finish in here and upstairs if you're done processing outside."

I didn't need the update, and I was more curious to discover what Dax found outdoors. Walking across the room to where he was standing, I held my hand next to his, hoping he'd slip me the cell phone. I made sure Gage wasn't paying any attention to us and casually asked, "Was there anything of interest out there?"

"Actually, there was. Peabody got plenty of photos and we bagged one black boot with an oversized buckle."

Did I hear him correctly? "Just one?"

He nodded. "And the insole had been ripped out and the laces tossed aside. Whoever took the boots were looking for something they thought was stashed inside."

I ran through a list of items that might be hidden in a

boot. A piece of paper like the one that had been in John's hand? A stone? A USB drive maybe? A key? But none of those made sense since as soon as the boot was turned upside down, they would have fallen out. Not looking at anyone in particular, I said, "Do you think they didn't have time to search both boots which is why they took one with them?"

"That's possible or maybe they found what they were searching for and wanted to keep it safe," Dax said.

Mac came over to us. "Someone is going to look out of place carrying one leprechaun boot down the street."

I was so intent on the tidbit, I failed to notice Gage had joined us too. "Just an additional odd puzzle piece for this case."

I needed my clue board as these thoughts circled my brain. Nothing was falling into place yet, and the chalkboard would help me find clarity. "I'm going back to the store. We'll talk later." Standing on my tiptoes, I bussed Gage's lips. "Be careful today."

He looked deep into my eyes. "You too."

W alking the short distance to my shop, the Cozy Nook Bookstore, Nikki stopped me before we reached the door. "Why would someone want to ruin my wedding? I keep going over it in my head. Could I have hurt someone and not realized it? I can't think of any reason why this would have happened."

I redirected her to the bench in the town park across from the store. We needed to take a few minutes to talk this out before giving our full attention to replacing her dress.

"I've done nothing but think about this since I walked

into the dining room. But my thinking changed when we discovered John Bailey dead. I don't believe for one minute this had anything to do with your wedding. It was a ruse to distract from what had really happened. Being focused on the dining room gave someone time to put distance between themselves and the B & B before he would be discovered. Remember, Katherine was out of the inn for a time, then we had tea. Only after all of that did we enter the dining room and it was another half hour before I went upstairs—well, maybe less, but you get the idea. There was plenty of time for all this to happen." I hadn't told her that someone came back in and took the boots. That was better left to reveal tonight when hopefully we'd have more information.

"But what about my dress? Why stuff it behind the tub?" She wiped away a lone tear that trickled down her cheek. "That was personal to me."

I took her icy hands in mine and rubbed them, hoping to comfort her before she really broke down. "Nikki, I don't have an answer for you yet, but you know me. We'll find out why."

She gave me a weak smile. "But first you're my maid of honor and we have a dress dilemma to fix." Standing up, she pulled me to my feet. "If anyone can fix this problem, it will be your aunt and my mother."

Iona and Mimi had been good friends before Nikki's parents had moved south, and I agreed with Nikki—between the two witches, anything was possible. "Then we'd better get inside and get to problem solving. But first" —I winked—"we should pop into William's bakery and get something sweet to go with tea."

Nikki laughed. "I won't fit into my dress, whatever we get, and neither will you."

I popped my hands on my hips. "I'll have you know that I've been limiting my visits to the Sweet Spot to once a week in your honor, and how much weight can I pack on in two days?"

She gave me a side-eye look as we crossed the park to the little bakery. "I guess that depends on how many pecan cinnamon buns you enjoy."

Giving her a shoulder bump, I said, "I promise after today I'll be good until the morning after your wedding, then all promises are null and void."

Nikki wrapped her arm around my waist, and I gave her a hug.

"You're the *best* best friend a girl could ever have."

"It takes one to be one." I grinned and opened the door where the smell of yeasty breads, cinnamon, and sweet icing greeted us. I groaned. Had I really just promised to eat only one for the next two days? Sweet stars. To date, this was the most challenging promise of my life.

"Hello, ladies." William was leaning against the cash register. "I haven't seen you in quite some time."

I jabbed a finger in Nikki's direction. "I need to fit into my dress for a certain bride's wedding."

He gave us a wide grin. "I thought you knew, all of my confections come without calories."

That was why I adored this man. Not only did he make the best pecan cinnamon rolls in town, but he was the sweetest, older gentleman around. His beloved wife Lulu passed away a few years ago, and on a semiregular basis, he went out to dinner with Gage and me. He was like our honorary grandfather, but not quite that old.

"I'll keep that in mind, but for today, I'd like a few scones, muffins, and of course the pecan cinnamon bun too.

We're having a brainstorming session at the bookstore and sugar fuels the brain cells."

He withdrew a white bakery box from under the counter and began to add an assortment of delectable treats when he paused. "Is there anything else I should include?"

"It's just Aunt Mimi and Nikki's mom, Iona."

His face brightened. "In that case, I need to add some lemon scones. They were always Iona's favorite. My Lulu always had them available knowing how much she loved them."

My heart sighed. "Just like how you're always taking care of us." I smiled at Nikki. "Even if she doesn't say it, Nikki is very fond of your pecan cinnamon rolls too."

William's eyes widened. "You can just whip up your own." He knew that Nikki was a kitchen witch like his beloved Lulu had been.

She leaned over the counter and cupped his cheek. "Baker to baker, you know someone else's treats are always better tasting than your own."

He glanced around. "Lulu is still the magic behind the recipes here. That's why they'll never change." Tapping the tip of his nose with his fingertip, he winked.

I glanced at Nikki. "A witch can leave gifts like that behind?"

It was her turn to laugh. "As Milo would say, Ms. Witch, you need to read your book."

Ugh, now Nikki was telling me to read *Practical Beginnings* too. I held up the corner of my tote bag. "I carry it with me now."

She laughed again. "Now you just need to open it on a more regular basis and read." She took the box from William and handed him some cash.

I pretended to stomp over to the door and looked at William. "Anything else I should read about?"

He grinned. "What do I know? I'm a non-magical, remember?"

And just like that the ball was back in my court.

Chapter 6
Gage

An hour after Lily and Nikki had left, I was walking out the front door of the B & B. The rest of the team had left fifteen minutes before, and I wanted to stay with Katherine a little longer so as not to leave her alone. Donnie White came sauntering up the front walk. I waited for him on the porch and said, "Hello, Donnie."

Surprise flitted through his eyes, but I noticed there wasn't concern lingering in them. "Hey, Gage. This is a surprise. Are you here helping to get the room ready for Nikki and Steve's wedding? From what Katherine has said, Nikki and Lily have everything under control. My wife feels like she can sit back and take the day off."

"I'm here in an official capacity." I waited for some type of concern to register but still nothing. He hadn't even asked about his wife. I knew there were all kinds of marriages, but if the roles had been reversed, the first thing I would have asked was if my wife was safe. Since he wasn't asking any questions and the air between us was woven with tension, I said, "Katherine is fine but one of your guests has died."

This guy was either one cool cucumber, or he already knew what had happened.

He shifted from one foot to the other. "Do you think we'll get sued?"

I narrowed my eyes and gave him my best glare, the one that usually made a suspect squirm. It was having the desired effect on Donnie.

"What? Am I supposed to ask a different question?"

"Don't you want to know who it was?"

He pushed back his dark knit cap from his head and shoved it into the pocket of his hoodie. "I'm guessing it was one of those guys who dresses up like an elf. They come every year for a couple of days and then disappear until next year. Since Katherine has kept the inn primarily empty due to the wedding reception, it's the only logical assumption." He tipped his head and gave me a challenging look. "Am I wrong?"

I thrust my chin upward. "No, you're correct. It was John Bailey from Boston."

A flicker of interest lit his dark eyes. "You don't say."

"Did you know him?"

He nodded. "Yeah, sure did. He's been coming here for at least five years. From what I heard, he and some friends checked in. They're all looking for a pot of gold at the end of a rainbow. But not many of those this time of year. Besides, if there's gold to be found, it will be at the bottom of the ocean. That's the reason why my business is so successful."

I swear he puffed up his chest. "Why's that?" I was pretty sure he was about to boast about his business, but occasionally, there might be a kernel of truth that was important.

"People pay to charter my boat to go treasure hunting. I have a crew of three besides me and we take people diving in search of Black Sam's treasure and anything else we might find."

"It was my understanding the pirate treasure was stored in a cave."

He tapped his temple with his gloved finger. "Sure, like three hundred years ago, but with oceans rising due to hurricanes or global warming, those trunks could have been swept out to sea and be almost anywhere now. So, from late spring to fall, we troll the coast of Maine. Wherever our customer wants to go, we'll take them."

"Where were you today? I know Katherine tried to call you and she left several voicemail messages."

"I was up to my elbows in maintenance on my boat. If you don't believe me, you can ask anyone on my crew. We were all there together except for a late lunch run."

I gestured to the door with a nod. "Katherine is pretty rattled. You might want to go easy on her tonight. And the dining room and bridal suite are off-limits until I say so." I knew I was laying it on kind of thick, but I never had been a fan of Donnie White. I always had the impression he was on the slippery side of business.

"Any particular reason or do I need to have my wife give me the gritty details?"

"The dining room was vandalized, and the suite is where we found the late Mr. Bailey."

His brow crinkled, and a frown set on his mouth. "What was he doing in there? That room is reserved for Nikki. And he always stays in a room overlooking the town square."

"We believe that's where he was killed." I said those words to see his reaction, but dang if it hadn't made a dent in his emotions.

"Huh. Well, who knows. Maybe now we'll have a leprechaun ghost. That would draw in a good crowd every year and help the bottom line for sure." He stuck his hand out and I allowed him to shake mine. "Thanks for being here with Katherine. I'm sure she appreciated the support, and I won't go near either room."

He stepped around me and pushed open the front door. I waited until he was inside and then another few moments just in case either he or Katherine came out. When I was certain they weren't, I walked down the stairs, my footsteps heavy, in the direction of my car. I withdrew my phone and noticed I had a missed call and a text from Lily.

Pizza tonight. See you when you get here. Xo

She must have thought I'd forget the plan. Rather than take the seconds to reach out, I got into my car and headed in the direction of her place, but then I made a detour and went to mine first. Brutus, my one-hundred-pound, over-sized lapdog, would need dinner, a potty break, and then I'd bring him with me. Nikki probably had Murphy, her retriever, with her and, of course, Milo would be stalking the guests. When he got tired of hovering, he'd curl up with Brutus since he always shared his table nibbles with Lily's familiar.

When I pulled into my driveway, I jotted off a text letting Lily know the plan. Before I got in the house, her reply was a happy face emoji. I whistled for my oversized baby as soon as the door opened, and he trotted into the front hall carrying a pillow from the couch. At least this one was intact as opposed to what he usually did to them.

I rubbed his ears. "Hey, boy, how was your day?"

A soft woof answered me. "Let's get you ready to go for a ride in the truck. A bio break, dinner, and then we're off."

I left the kitchen door open as Brutus dashed outside to

the backyard. While I moved around the room, I let my mind wander to the case. First, I thought of how Lily had become a magnet for trouble. It seemed to coincide with her discovering she was a witch. When Flora Gray, the head librarian, was killed, it was the same day Lily got hit in the head with her family's book of magic and that's when she discovered Milo was her familiar and he talked. Shortly after that, Teddy Roberts died, then when she was reading tea leaves, Dean Hartley was killed, and of course there was the newspaper reporter at Halloween. After dinner or even tomorrow, I'd touch base with Mom and ask her if it was possible that Lily's newly discovered powers could have somehow tipped the scales out of balance.

I felt a large, cold, and wet nose nuzzle my hand, and I knelt down. "Hey, boy. A couple really great things came out of the last few months. I adopted you, and Lily and I are engaged. If the scales did get out of whack, I think they went in my favor for sure."

In response, he gave me a big, sloppy kiss on my cheek before knocking me onto my back and lying on top of me. Laughing, I felt my life was pretty close to perfection. I managed to get out from under the beastie and put his bowl on the floor. He inhaled it and trotted to the door, ready to hit the road which had become our new routine.

"Brutus, you keep me on my toes." The moment I opened the front door, he dashed to the driver's side of the truck. My thoughts drifted back to Donnie, and why he hadn't answered his phone or been concerned for his wife the minute he learned about John Bailey? It was almost as if he had known what had happened.

Donnie would have known about the door leading into the dining room. Heck, he probably even had a key to it since there were no signs of it being forced. And in the course of a workday, he never once touched base with his wife? I chuckled to myself. I needed Lily's chalkboard to lay this all out. Starting with, why did our unknown person leave one leprechaun boot and take the other?

I entered Lily's house, and the kitchen was a hive of activity. As usual, I was the last to arrive. Dax and Steve were adding a leaf to the table. Peabody was tossing a salad. Mac was handling drinks. Nikki was whipping up some kind of dessert, and Lily was feeding the four-legged family members. Brutus nudged me aside and hurried over to Lily who immediately kissed the top of his head before lifting her eyes to meet mine. Despite the happy chaos, her look was meant just for me. She mouthed hello and blew me a kiss. It was more personal than her walking over to greet me which would draw everyone's attention.

Dax noticed me standing in the doorway. "'Bout time you showed up. We need a couple more chairs."

"Sorry I'm late. I got sidetracked, and before you ask"—I saw Lily straighten and look directly at me—"I'll tell you all about it after we eat. I'm starving."

"Then you'd better get chairs, or you can sit on the floor," Dax joked.

Our group consisted of three witches and four non-magicals. Two of those didn't know witches existed much less lived in Pembroke Cove, and we needed to keep it quiet. So even if Lily could make chairs appear, it probably wasn't a good idea.

Dax and I went and grabbed the chairs, and once they were arranged, I said, "What happened about finding a dress? Did Mimi or Iona have any ideas?"

Nikki looked at me. "Mimi and Mom listened to what happened and said they would work on it. I'm hoping we hear from them after dinner. If not, I'm not sure what I'll do."

Lily gave her a one-armed hug. "You know between them it will be a happy ending. Try not to worry."

Sharon said, "Lily's right, Nikki. Mimi Michaels knows every talented person in Maine. It will work out."

Nikki nodded. "With those," she paused and then said, "ladies, all things are possible."

I knew she meant they'd use their magic, if necessary, to get her a dress.

M ilo, Murphy, and Brutus were stretched out, relaxing with full bellies, and we were all gathered around the table. I had a slice of pizza loaded with everything, poised for my first bite when Lily folded her hands on the tabletop and said, "What happened when you were leaving the B & B?"

I was so close to getting something to eat. "I ran into Donnie coming in as I was leaving." Resigned to sharing all the details, I set the pizza back on my plate. "You know Katherine was trying to reach him during the afternoon, and when I mentioned it, he said he was doing boat maintenance and didn't hear the phone ring."

Lily pursed her lips, and she looked at her clue board which was currently blank. "So, the man never checked his phone during the day. What was his demeanor when you saw him? Concerned? Anxious? Anything to indicate he knew something had happened?"

"He was just a guy coming home from work. But the strange thing is when I told him what happened, his first comment wasn't concern for his wife. He asked if I thought they'd get sued. Even when I talked about the vandalism, he was still nonchalant about the entire thing."

Lily jabbed a cucumber slice with her fork and held it up like a wand, waving it in the air. "Let me get this straight. Someone dying in the same building where his wife was, by herself, did nothing to rattle him?" She shook her head. "What kind of husband is that?"

Giving Steve a long, hard look before she smiled, Lily said, "For the record, you better be the best husband in the world to Nikki and not take even so much as a single word from Donnie's husband manual."

He clasped Nikki's hand. "You don't have a thing to worry about. Nikki always has and always will come first in my life."

She leaned over and kissed him. "And you me."

Lily nodded. "Now that I have that out there with witnesses, let's finish our dinner so I can start the board. There are a lot of floating pieces that make no sense whatsoever."

Conversation turned to Mac and his baby daughter. "You should see her. Amanda is crawling all over the place and pulling herself up. She's the smartest baby ever. Even Margaret agrees."

I chuckled. "Amanda must take after your wife."

Peabody laughed. "Or me."

Dax looked around the circle of friends. "Maybe I should jump onto this train and say she takes after her new uncle Dax."

Mac picked up his mug and tapped it to his. "I'll do one better. Amanda has a little bit of all of you in her. After all, we spend so much time together, I think you wore off on me."

Camaraderie filled the room, but I had one eye on Lily, and her mind was elsewhere. If I had to guess, she was walking through everything that had happened earlier today, just as I had done, but there were so many missing pieces.

Lily looked up, her eyes wide. "Wait a minute. What about Bailey's friends? Have you interviewed them yet?"

"No. Katherine said they had gone treasure hunting but didn't know where, and they haven't come back to the B & B as of an hour ago. But I asked her to call me when they showed up."

Mac pushed his plate aside. "I have a feeling we're going back on the clock tonight."

"No, you and Peabody should enjoy yourselves. There will be a lot happening tomorrow." I glanced at Dax who held up his mug. "Ginger ale. I had a feeling tonight was going to be a long one."

Lily eased back her chair. "Well then, we've got no time to lose. Let's put our heads together and be prepared. Once the interviews happen, hopefully we'll be able figure out who, why, and when."

Chapter 7
Lily

Once the table was cleared, I filled the chalkboard with all we knew so far about the case. Our victim, the missing then found wedding dress, the leprechaun boot, the vandalism, and Donnie being MIA during the afternoon. "Does anyone know if I've overlooked anything at this point?"

Nikki snapped her fingers, and it drew my attention away from the board. "Your aunt's cutlery is missing."

"Are you sure?" I withdrew my phone from my jeans and scrolled through the pictures I had taken. I could feel Gage's eyes on me, but I didn't look up. I said, "Where was it supposed to be? On the tables or still in a box?"

"When I was there earlier, I set a few pieces near the plates to see what it would look like." She extended her hand to me, and I gave her the phone and looked over her shoulder. "They're gone, and"—she tapped the screen to make the image bigger—"see the wooden box was right behind that short stack of plates."

I passed the phone to Gage. "On top of destruction, there's a little larceny thrown in for good measure."

"I'm going to send this to myself," he said.

I went back to the clue board and wrote down *missing cutlery*. Aunt Mimi wasn't going to be happy about that since it had been in our family for generations. But I wasn't about to mention its real value in front of Nikki and Steve; they had enough on their plates. I smiled inwardly at the poor pun.

"On to the crime upstairs." I turned the board around so there was a side for new information.

John Bailey, Boston, victim. I scrawled across the top.

No boots

Bathtub

Treasure hunter – three friends MIA?

I looked at my friends. "What else do we know about John?"

Gage said, "He's been coming to Pembroke Cove for at least five years in search of Black Sam's supposed treasure. And per a printed flyer at the inn, the legend states it can only be found around St. Patrick's Day."

"Where did you see a flyer?"

Gage said, "When I was sitting with Katherine, I noticed it on the side table."

"Huh." I couldn't remember seeing it but there had been a lot happening at the time.

Dax looked around the group. "I think our victim was caught off guard since there was no sign of a struggle between him and his attacker."

"Could he have just fallen back and hit his head?" I asked, more to myself than to the group.

"If that was the case, what about the boots being in the dining room and then gone? Someone took them, so it has to be connected," Sharon said.

"And they came in after Lily had already seen them." Mac casually tossed that out.

I saw the flash of worry flit across Gage's face. I know what he was thinking. "I'll be fine. There is so much to get done for the wedding I won't have time to follow up on any clues." My attempt to reassure Gage and my friends was met with a look of disbelief that was like a fan wave at a baseball game.

Milo perked his head up and grumbled, "My dear witch, Detective Cutie doesn't buy that for one second." I frowned and just shook my head.

Dax smothered a grin. As a witch he too could understand what Milo said and Nikki nodded. "Right."

Gage looked between Dax and Nikki. He threw his hands up and let them drop back to his lap. With a sigh, he said, "I give up."

Sharon, Mac, and Steve also couldn't understand what Milo had just said, after all it was a witch thing. But Gage knew Milo had imparted some clever remark since they usually were. But I loved my fur ball despite his snarky ways.

Steve held up his glass in Gage's direction and grinned. "Welcome to my world."

Mac said, "Did Peabody and I miss something?"

Gage got up from the table and began to clear it. "Nothing important." His cell phone chirped, and he pulled it from the holder on his belt. Without looking up, he said, "It's from Katherine. Dylan O'Hara, Arthur Nolan, and Shay Keegan have just gotten back to the B & B." He set the empty pizza box on the counter. "Mac and Peabody, call it a day, and Dax, you're with me."

I put the chalk down. "I'm coming too."

Gage shook his head. "No. This is a murder investigation, and I appreciate all that you're doing but if one of these men killed Bailey, I don't want you near them. They may already know who you are."

"But..." I sputtered.

"I promise I'll fill you in on the details, but you need to call your aunt and tell her what happened about the missing cutlery, and then there is a bride who needs her best friend's help in wrapping up the details for her wedding."

Steve stood. "Gage, are you sure we can use the room for the reception? I could make some calls and see if we can use the grange hall if that would take the pressure off."

Gage looked at Nikki before turning his attention to Steve. "As long as I feel the scene is cleared, you can move ahead with the reception as planned." He gave Nikki his killer smile that always made me feel like everything was going to work out perfectly. "Even if we have to work all night tomorrow, we will pull it together. Come four o'clock Saturday afternoon, we'll be celebrating the newest Mr. and Mrs."

Dax had crossed the room and handed Gage his jacket. "Thanks for dinner, Lily." He gave me a wink. I took that as he would fill me in on any interesting tidbits if Gage didn't. At least I hoped he did.

Gage put his hands on my shoulders and pulled me close. He tenderly kissed my lips before saying, "I know you want to be in the thick of this, but she needs you more." He bobbed his head in Nikki's direction, and I knew he was right. "I'll call you when I get home."

He tapped his leg for Brutus to come with him, and I said, "Let him stay here while you do your detective thing. You can swing by on your way home."

He laughed softly. "Is that your way of making sure I fill you in on the case?"

I tipped my head to the side and hoped I wore my sweet, innocent smile. "Only if you want to."

He pointed to my cell phone. "Call Mimi."

I followed him out the door. "Take good notes."

He held up a hand in a sort of wave. "Yes, ma'am."

I went back inside. Gage was right on a couple of things. Aunt Mimi needed to be told about the fate of her dishes and cutlery, and with any luck, she would have come up with an idea about a wedding dress.

A unt Mimi sailed through the back door, slamming it shut behind her. I sat up straight, startled at her entrance. I got up and she pointed to my chair.

"Sit. You've had a rough day." Her gaze took in both me and Nikki. "Both of you look like you've been stirred in the cauldron since I saw you earlier this afternoon. Did something else happen?"

"No, just trying to figure out where to go from here."

She bent over and scratched Milo's ears. "How are they really doing, Milo?"

With a flick of his tail, he purred. "Better now that you're here."

She looked around and crossed to the living room. "Where's Steve and Gage? I thought for sure they'd be here too."

Nikki said, "Steve took Murphy home, but I knew he wanted to give us some space so that we could talk about the wedding dress."

I wanted to interject that it was only after Nikki promised to call when she was ready to leave. He wanted to pick her up which was the sweetest thing since they both had a difficult day, but I liked that he was being very considerate.

"Will Iona be here shortly?" Aunt Mimi waved her hand, and the chair slid out from the table.

At the mention of her mother, Nikki hung her head. "I know she's upset after I told her what had happened to the dress."

My aunt placed a comforting hand on Nikki's. "She would want to be here to help us resolve this little speed bump. Why don't you go into the other room and give her a call and see what time she's coming? We'll wait." She gave me a pointed look as if I needed to support her statement.

"Nikki, call your mom. Aunt Mimi's right. Iona wants to help us figure out what you'll wear to your wedding."

With slumped shoulders and her face pinched tight, she got up from the table and walked into the other room. Milo swished his tail and followed her. My familiar could be a great comfort when the mood struck him, and he was fond of Nikki. He'd be sitting right beside her while she talked to her mom.

Once she was in the living room, my aunt leaned forward. "Since this afternoon, I've been recalling what you told me about the inn, and I can't believe you found another body."

I got up. "Tea?" I filled the kettle and put it on the stove to heat. I selected a blend of Mom's that was for calm, clear thinking.

"Lily." She said my name softly. "I don't like that you're the person who keeps stumbling onto these crimes."

I leaned against the kitchen counter and folded my arms over my midsection. "Aunt Mimi, it hasn't been the high point of my year, but for some reason it keeps happening, so

I think it must be fate that I do. Besides, you know how much I love solving puzzles."

"No one in our family has ever been in this position before." She drummed her fingertips on the smooth wood tabletop. "But as with all things in life, there are reasons that we may not understand."

"Exactly." I took a deep breath since I hadn't told her over the phone about the rest of what had happened today. "I'm afraid I have some upsetting news."

She turned in the chair, not saying a word so that I had her undivided attention.

"The plates, glasses, and cutlery that you and Nate brought over for the reception, well, a bunch were broken when whoever it was trashed the dining room, and I'm sorry to be the one to tell you, but the gold cutlery is missing."

She didn't blink but stared at me as if she was trying to comprehend what I had just said. I knew the cutlery was priceless. "Can you cast a locator spell to find it?"

"Of course I can, but I find it hard to comprehend that someone would deliberately want to cause Nikki and Steve so much unhappiness days before their wedding. First damaging her dress and leaving it at the scene of the murder and then breaking dishes and stealing some forks and spoons. This is outrageous."

My aunt was taking this much better than I had expected. The teakettle began to chirp, and I poured the boiling water over the loose-leaf tea infuser. Nikki came back into the room carrying Milo in her arms, stroking his head. My familiar was purring like a loud motorboat. I smiled, proud that he had worked his calming magic on her.

"My mom will be here in about ten minutes." She gently placed Milo on the floor. "Mimi, I can tell by the fire in your eyes that Lily told you the rest of the news."

She opened her arms to Nikki. "You're not to worry about a thing. I'll fix the dishes and we'll find the missing flatware. I guarantee you one thing. Whoever did this will be very sorry they messed with this witch."

I joined the hug and said, "A better statement would be *these witches*."

Aunt Mimi held us a little tighter. "You are absolutely right."

After a couple more minutes of drawing strength from each other, I stepped back. "I'm sure the tea is ready. Let me get cups."

"Do you have any cookies in your pantry, Lily?" My aunt's eyes twinkled.

"I happen to have some that Nikki brought over yesterday."

She said, "I'll get them."

Aunt Mimi said, "I'll answer the door." She swept from the kitchen in the direction of the front door, and I touched Nikki's arm.

"Are you really doing okay?"

Nikki gave me a tight smile. "Someday I'll look back on this and laugh. But for now, it's something we'll deal with. On a brighter note, I forgot to tell you I've perfected the flavor profile for the cake, filling, and frosting."

Rubbing my hands together, I said, "Tell me, I'm dying to know."

She shook her head and with a small laugh, she said, "Nope. It's going to be a surprise. And while I was in a creative mood, I jotted down some ideas for your wedding cake too."

I held up my hand in a stop motion. "I'm enjoying being engaged, and I'm not in any rush to walk down the aisle.

You and Steve have been a couple for years. Give me and Gage some time to enjoy this new stage of our relationship."

Nikki gave me a quick hug. "Take all the time you need, but know I'm ready to fulfill my duties as your matron of honor and cake baker extraordinaire."

"I'll keep that in mind, but let's concentrate on one wedding at a time."

Aunt Mimi and Iona hurried into the room. Iona was carrying a garment bag over her arm. She kissed Nikki's cheek and then mine.

"My sweet girl, I have the most wonderful news. You'll never guess what I brought with me from home."

"Your dress for the wedding?" Nikki looked at me, her eyebrows knitted together, confusion filling her eyes. "I hope."

"Well, yes, but this is better." She hung the garment bag on a cabinet doorknob and unzipped it. "Close your eyes, sweetie pie."

"Mom, I really don't feel like..." She threw up her hands. "Fine." She plunked into a chair and closed her eyes.

When Iona folded back the garment bag, I gasped. "Nikki, you need to look at this."

She twirled in the chair as she opened her eyes. "Mom, how did you get my dress?"

"Well, it's not an exact duplicate, but this was the dress I wore when I married your father. When you picked out your gown, I didn't want to tell you how close it was to mine since I knew you wanted your own dress. But my intuition told me to bring it."

Nikki burst into tears, and Iona knelt down next to her. "Please tell me these are tears of joy?"

She hugged her mom and then looked at me, her cheeks

damp and eyes sparkling like diamonds. "Lily. The happiness meter just went off the charts."

I clapped my hands together and grinned. "I'll let a certain detective know he can keep the other dress for as long as he needs."

Chapter 8
Lily

After I hung up from talking with Gage, I grinned at Nikki, Iona, and my aunt as I looked around my kitchen table. "What's next, more tea and dessert?"

"In a couple of minutes, Lily." Nikki turned in her chair and looked at her mom. "I'm a little confused. If the dress I picked out at the bridal salon and yours were so much alike, why didn't you remind me?"

Iona tipped her head and smiled. "When you didn't realize the similarity, I wasn't going to bring it up and cause you any embarrassment. This is the happiest time of your life, and all I want is for you to create lasting memories. Spending the day with you shopping was a wonderful part of our journey as mother and daughter." She took Nikki's hands. "However, in light of the circumstances, everything is turning out exactly as it should. If you had my dress in that dining room and it had gotten caught up in that poor man's death..." Her voice trailed off until she gave us all a bright smile. "It's all worked out as it was destined to be."

Aunt Mimi said, "Iona's right. Now, shall we focus on the next few days and not the past?"

My aunt's outlook was always sunny, and I walked over and hugged her from behind. "Thank you for being you." I kissed her on the cheek and straightened up. "Now, let's get back to planning a wedding."

With a point of her finger, Aunt Mimi had the water heating in the kettle again so we could have a fresh pot of tea. Nikki opened my cabinet doors and was looking at the almost empty shelves. I hoped she would be able to concoct a sweet treat from what little was in there.

"When do you think we can get into the dining room at the B & B?" Aunt Mimi asked. "I want to be in the room when I do the locating spell for the cutlery since it was the last place it had been."

"Gage said he thought sometime late morning. I figured we can have you find the utensils, have Nate bring over more dishes, and with some wand work, we can get the place spotless pretty quickly." I placed the teacups on the table and then added the honey pot and sugar bowl. I couldn't stop thinking about the original wedding dress. Why would someone take it and then hide it behind the tub? How was it connected to the murder, and why did someone take the box of eating utensils?

A poke on my arm drew me out of my thoughts.

Nikki said, "Can you stop thinking about whatever it is" —she pointed to my clue board—"and let's talk about the wedding day and timing for it all."

I gave one last look to the board, knowing I could dwell on those questions when everyone left for the evening. With a bit of luck, when Gage stopped by to pick up Brutus, he'd fill me in on what had happened when he interviewed John Bailey's friends from Boston.

Flashing Nikki a wide smile, I hopefully conveyed I was all in for organizing the wedding day events. "Let's make that list. All I need is my laptop so I can print off copies for all concerned."

Iona chuckled. "We need lists?"

I placed a hand on my chest in mock horror, hoping my face held the same expression. "Didn't you get my emails and memos on the schedule?"

Laughing, she said, "I didn't memorize them."

With a wave of my hand, I produced a copy of the old schedule and handed it to her. "As maid of honor, it is my sacred duty to make sure the bride, aka Nikki, doesn't get one worry line on her beautiful face before the big day."

Aunt Mimi clapped her hands. "Bravo!"

It was a simple feat, having the paper float up from the counter into my hand. It wasn't that big of a deal, but at least it was a spell I had mastered. Progress.

Nikki pulled out a chair and sat down. "Mom, you might as well come to terms that I did not become a bridezilla, but Lily, on the other hand, has taken her duty as the MOH to an entirely new level of organization. She's more like a wedding planner and best friend all rolled into one."

I puffed up. "That was a lovely way to say I've become totally focused on every detail, right down to how many after-dinner mints are tied up in cellophane with emerald-green ribbon."

Aunt Mimi arched her brow. "Are you saying you put together the favors for the event? And did you do it with magic or without?"

I picked up the teapot and filled the four cups. Making her wait a couple of moments was fun. "It just so happens I was reading my big book on magic when the thought of a spell crossed my mind. And sure enough, the pages began to flip and there it was, a spell for getting all kinds of wedding tasks completed. It was a gift from all the Michaels' witches that came before me who also had been a maid of honor."

Aunt Mimi clasped her hands together and beamed. "Thank the sun, moon, and stars. Our newest witch is using all the tools in her cauldron."

I felt warmth creep over my cheeks at my aunt's praise. It wasn't from embarrassment but happiness. I had shown her I was taking my lessons seriously and was determined to be a good—no, great—witch.

* * *

I was under the covers in bed with a romance novel on my lap and Milo snuggled in close and Brutus lying on the other side when my phone buzzed. Gage's picture came up on the screen and I answered on speakerphone.

"Hi, Lily, did I wake you?"

I glanced at the clock, surprised to discover it was after midnight. "No, I was reading. How did things go tonight?"

"Meh."

That response was unlike Gage. He was great at interviewing people, moving slowly with a lot of pauses in the conversation so people were happy to spill all the little details.

"It was bad?"

"Of course, the friends seem to be in shock which is understandable, and they all have an alibi for most of the day away from the B & B. Of course, we'll check that out in the morning. But they didn't have a good explanation of why John Bailey wasn't with them. They all tap-danced around the same questions. It was almost like they had rehearsed their answers ahead of time."

"But you said their reaction to the news about his death seemed genuine."

"That's part of the issue. If they're not involved in the murder, then there is more at play here, and I'm at a loss to know what it is."

I wasn't about to defend three people I had never met, so I said, "Could it be possible you're just so tired, physically and emotionally, that you can't sort out the line between grief and hiding something?"

He didn't speak for a moment. "What do you mean about the emotion part?"

"Our best friends are getting married at the inn, and people who we love had things either damaged or plain stolen for no apparent reason. I'm drained from today, and I'm sure you are too. It's natural when it becomes personal."

"True. But this case is already bugging me, and I can't put my finger on it."

I knew exactly how he was feeling since I was in the same boat. "I get it. I've been mulling over how the items for the wedding tie back to everything else. Why the missing boot? Why the bridal suite? I'm sure Nikki and Steve aren't connected. It must be a random act."

"In police work we believe nothing is random, so we'll find the connection. It might take some time."

Oh stars, was he trying to tell me something I didn't want to hear? "Gage, what aren't you saying?"

"It's nothing."

Two could play his wait and listen game. So, I sat, impatiently waiting, smoothing my blankets.

Milo opened one eye and glared at me. "And what are you doing?"

I put a finger over my lips and pointed to my phone.

"Your detective and you are being lovey-dovey on the phone? Gross."

I shook my head no. I gave him a hard look, hoping he'd stop talking. Even if Gage couldn't understand Milo, he'd be able to tell by the sounds of meowing that we were having a conversation.

"Look, do you want to know what's bothering me?" It was easy to hear the edge in his voice.

"Yes." I held my breath, knowing this probably wasn't going to be productive, but he needed to get whatever it was off his chest.

"The person who snuck in and took the boot did it while you were there, and that person might be the killer. You were in danger. Again."

Now it was out in the open. I had a way of finding trouble even when I was trying to solve a puzzle—or as Gage would refer to it, a crime.

Keeping my voice soft and reassuring, I said, "You forget I had secured the doors from the dining room to the rest of the building. If the person had come in through the front door carrying one or both boots, I have the skills to protect me and Katherine if needed." I softened my voice even further. "I've mastered the protection spell."

A ragged breath seeped over the phone line. "Lily, it scares me when I think of all that happened there right under your wand. I couldn't bear it if anything happened to you. Not after all the wasted time we spent dancing around our feelings for each other."

"Take several deep breaths and close your eyes for me. Pretend that you're sitting next to me on the sofa holding my hand." I continued to encourage him to really focus.

"Even though we're not physically together, can you feel my touch, the warmth of my hand in yours?"

"I do."

"Gage, we have something special. We've always been connected to each other. Which is why the first person I learned to protect was you. Do you remember at the library, I wrapped you in a protection spell?"

He laughed softly. "I do and left yourself exposed to danger, all to save me."

"I came through that just like I will always come through any challenge unharmed. And if I need you, we're connected."

"I just don't like it."

I waited for half a minute. "Are you asking me to stop living my life? I can't help what situations I walk into."

"No." His voice was firm. "I would never want you to be anyone you're not, but I can wish that you'd always be safe and never in danger."

My heart melted, and I touched the black tourmaline and amethyst necklace Aunt Mimi had given me months ago. It was to provide additional protection when I needed it. At the moment it was cool to the touch which always meant I was fine.

"Sweetheart, this is how our lives are going to be. You chase the bad guys and toss them in jail, and I track down clues and help where I can. I don't go looking for danger. Sometimes it has found me, but out of all the women you could have as a silent partner in crime, aren't you glad it's me?"

"Lady, you slay me with your logic." His voice was lighter now. "What new spell are you working on?"

He had to go and ruin a perfectly nice conversation by

mentioning my book, *Practical Beginnings*. Milo lifted his head and I swear he smirked at the question.

He wasn't pressuring me, but it was a common question since I discovered I was a late-blooming witch. I still had so much to catch up on. "I'm pleasure reading tonight."

"Then I'm going to let you go back to your book, and we'll see each other tomorrow at the B & B. What time do you think you'll get there?"

"Can we clean up the room and get it reset?"

"I'll release it around ten. But what are you going to do about the table settings?"

I smiled. "Aunt Mimi will find the missing items using a locator spell and Nate will bring over plates and whatever else is needed. And before you ask, as soon as she knows where the stuff has been stashed, she'll let you know first so you can do your thing."

He chuckled. "Wow. You know the first comments that spring to mind."

I rolled my eyes even though he couldn't see them. It still set up the possibility for a quick retort. "You're predictable when it comes to your job. Like don't touch anything; don't go off on your own investigating; be careful."

Now he snorted. "It's good to know that you've actually retained my standard lines. Not that you always execute them in the same manner in which they were said."

"Oh, Gage. I'm doing the best I can. I'm inquisitive by nature. This isn't new news."

"We're not going down this conversational road tonight. We have a busy and fun few days ahead of us. Oh, and can you bring Brutus with you tomorrow? I'm sure he's sound asleep on your bed."

I reached over and patted the one-hundred-pound pup. "That he is."

"I love you, Lily. Sleep well."

"I love you, Gage."

After we disconnected, I clicked off the lamp and the weak light came in from the moon as I ran my hand down the length of Milo's warm, silky soft body.

He shifted to a seated position. "Are you thinking about what Gage said, how close you were to the person who stole the boot?"

"I should have thought to secure the entire inn, not just the doors." Milo bumped my hand out of his way and perched on my stomach.

He said, "Think about that. If you had, whoever it was would have been trapped inside with you and who knows what might have happened. Katherine is a non-magical person so it wouldn't be like you could start casting protection spells or much of anything else for that matter. The goal of a witch is to fly under the radar."

I cupped my hands around his tiny face. "Speaking of flying, when do I get to learn?"

He stretched out across my body and yawned. "Your book will show you when it's time, but you have to keep reading and practicing the spells as they are presented to you. Everything comes in due course, and magic can never be rushed. It's like fishing or even exploring for buried pirate treasure. It will happen when it happens."

In the dim light of the moon, he closed his eyes, and soon the sounds of him snoring was lulling me to sleep. Tomorrow, I needed to talk with the friends of the deceased and Donnie White. The last thing I remember thinking about was Aunt Mimi casting a spell to set a few things right. Nikki would be thrilled to get everything back on track for her big day.

Chapter 9
Gage

The next morning when I drove down the street, I wasn't really surprised to see a blue and white Mini Cooper parked in front of the Pembroke Cove B & B. I shook my head. "Lily." How had she gotten here ahead of me when I left my place earlier than normal? Obviously, it wasn't early enough.

I parked in front of her car and before getting out, I looked up the street and in my rearview mirror. I had the feeling I was being watched but I couldn't see anyone. Once I was standing on the sidewalk, I looked around again as a prickling sensation raced down my spine. I walked up the steps, scanning the windows to see if anyone was lingering. But not so much as a curtain fluttered.

As I entered the old inn, the smell of coffee greeted me as if I was expected, but Katherine must have set breakfast out for her guests. As I entered the main room, I saw Lily sitting with the men I had spoken to last night; Dylan, Arthur, and Shay were at a table enjoying a cup of what I presumed was coffee. She was smiling and chatting amiably and didn't even acknowledge my presence. That little witch was doing her version of questioning the suspects. I knew there was no way she could compromise the investigation, but it was apparent to her I wasn't going to divulge information. Instead of lingering in the room, I walked down the hall in search of Peabody or Mac—maybe even Dax might be here before me.

The dining room was dark behind the glass door. I turned the knob, and it was locked. Instead of waiting to see who might show up, I walked back through the main room and took the stairs to the second floor. I intended to go back to where we had found Mr. Bailey. Since there was no evidence of a struggle, could it have been an accident? Maybe he could have slipped being in socks, fell back and hit his head, and being alone, he died without anyone knowing he was in the room.

At least that was a theory Dylan had suggested. He had said John was in search of a map to where Black Sam's treasure was buried and even mentioned he was friends with a local treasure hunter who had been helping them.

I paused outside the suite door and wondered again about Donnie White. After all, he owned a treasure hunting boat, and his wife ran the inn. But that fit together much too conveniently, and would he really kill a man who was staying at his wife's place of business? I thought not. Besides, he might be a greedy businessman, preying on the gullible to hunt for water-logged treasure, but what he did wasn't a crime.

I noticed Peabody coming out of the suite's bathroom.

"Morning, Detective. Did you see Lily downstairs?"

I gave her a rueful smile. "I did. She's busy chatting with our victim's travel buddies."

Nodding, Peabody said, "Lily was here when I arrived, and she was sitting and leafing through a magazine, looking all casual, but you know her. She had her questions all practiced in her head. Those men didn't know what was going to hit them."

It was easy to smile as Peabody described my girlfriend to a T. I wondered what kind of information she was able to extract from the friends. "You got that right." I stepped into the suite and looked around. Fingerprint powder dusted every wooden surface.

"We haven't found anything else," she noted.

"What do you think? Is it possible it was a tragic accident?" I crossed into the bathroom and scanned the room again, taking in every detail, but nothing screamed clue to me.

"My instincts are telling me no. There is the wedding dress put behind the tub. If he had leaned over to do that, he would have fallen forward. Where he connected with the cast iron was in the back of the head."

I knew all of this, but it was good to go over everything again with fresh eyes. "I'm going to release the dining room for the wedding reception unless you're not finished in there."

She rested her hand on her wide belt buckle. "We should do one more sweep of the room just to be sure. Under normal circumstances, I'd suggest we keep it secured, but I get that Nikki and Steve would be disappointed to postpone their wedding."

I nodded. "Other than someone stealing the boots and breaking some dishes, it really wasn't that big of a deal."

"You're forgetting Mimi's gold cutlery."

I hated that she had to remind me. "Mimi and Iona are coming by in a bit. The flatware service she let Nikki borrow was valuable. I'll see if she minds that we're moving forward with the wedding. After all she's a part of our investigation too. My guess is she won't." I thought for a minute, then asked, "Peabody, why do you think the wedding dress was removed from downstairs, ripped, and left up here?"

"I honestly don't know yet. But as with all cases, we'll know by the time we close the file on it."

I made a mental note to ask Lily what her thoughts were on the dress. For the life of me I just couldn't figure out what it had to do with John Bailey. "Anything I need to take a look at before I join Lily?"

"No, in fact, I'll head down to the dining room and when you see Dax or Mac show up, send them in too. It'll be quicker to do one last check with more sets of eyes."

"Agreed." I went down the back stairs and paused halfway. Dialing the medical examiner's office, I wondered if EL had established a time of death.

"ME's office. Dawson here." His tone was brisk as always.

"Hi. It's Gage Erikson."

"Detective, you're calling about my report on John Bailey?"

I liked how he never was one to beat around the bush and got right down to business—well, except when we were on the same team for the annual softball charity event. Then he was the prankster in the group. "Yes, any chance you determined time of death yet?"

"Yes, it was between ten and eleven yesterday morning. And before you ask, it was a blow to the back of the head, but it wasn't from the tub. His neck was broken, and my working theory is a skillet or pot of some kind."

I began to imagine how that would play out. "Cookware? That was not what I thought you were going to say."

"Think about it this way. If the object was swung at the correct angle and speed and it connected with the head as it did in this case, it could break the neck and death would be almost instant. Or the force of the impact would propel the victim back, and if he hadn't suffered from a broken neck, cracking his skull against the tub would have finished the job."

He painted an excellent picture of what might have happened. "Thanks for the update, EL." I sank to a stair tread. So, if Katherine left the B & B to do errands, what time did she leave? There was an altercation upstairs and Bailey was dead. Did he have his boots on when he died and they were removed? And the bigger question is, why take a pair of leprechaun boots?

I double-checked my notes, and Katherine had been vague about the time she left and returned. That was my first question when I saw her. The next was for my mom and Mimi. Was there any way to cast a spell so any evidence that might still be in the room remained untouched during the wedding? It was a long shot but the only one I had to let the reception take place so everyone would be happy.

L ily was sitting alone in the lobby when I got downstairs. I was slipping my small notepad in my jacket pocket, and her eyes widened with interest. I bent over and kissed her cheek. "How's your sleuthing been?"

"Interesting and yours?"

"Confusing." I sat in the chair opposite her. I wasn't ready to share all the questions I had. Instead, I said, "Care to tell me what you discovered?"

Her mischievous smile tugged at the corner of her lips

and lingered in her sable-brown eyes. "Possibly, if you tell me what happened upstairs?"

Since she hadn't asked about the medical examiner's report, I decided no harm could come from telling her that Peabody hadn't found anything new. "Peabody's upstairs, as you know since you were here when she arrived." I quirked a brow. "Which, I'd like to know, what time did you arrive?"

"Just before seven. I figured the treasure hunters would get an early start even though their friend died, and I was right. Those men are single-minded in finding the gold." She wagged a finger in my direction. "You're going first, remember?"

I couldn't help but smile; she knew all my tricks. "The only fingerprints she's finding are from the cleaning person and Katherine."

"And how does she know for certain that's whose prints they are?"

The subject of prints had never come up before. "Prior to moving to Pembroke Cove, Peabody was a highly trained fingerprint examiner. She compared prints she found in the room yesterday to both Katherine and the other lady and they matched. So far there aren't any others in the bedrooms."

A frown settled over Lily's bow-like mouth. "I was hoping for something."

"We all were. There isn't even anything in the bathroom. Either the perp never touched anything or wiped the surface as they left the room."

She narrowed her eyes and nodded. "I'm betting on the latter. There is no way a crime could have been committed, or even poor John Bailey going into the room, and never touching a single doorknob or surface. It's just not logical."

She was right, and I wished I had put that piece of the

puzzle neatly into place. But maybe I was overthinking this case. It had definitely gotten under my skin whereas others hadn't.

"Have you spoken to EL Dawson yet?"

Dang, it was like she could read my mind. "Yes, the preliminary report is ready, and John Baily died midmorning from a broken neck."

Her hand flew to her mouth. "That poor man, falling into the tub and breaking his neck."

I debated for a fraction of a second on telling her everything, but the last time I withheld a vital piece of information, she got very upset with me. The best way to keep her from going off on her own investigation without support was to be as transparent as possible while still maintaining confidentiality for the case.

"He was hit on the back of the head by a skillet or a pot of some kind."

She slid forward on her chair, her eyebrow arched in a quizzical gesture. "A pot? Maybe it was the cauldron where the leprechaun keeps his gold."

"Sweetheart, leprechauns aren't witches so they didn't use cauldrons, but they did have some kind of pot." I withdrew my notebook and jotted a note to look up what was common for the Irish to use for cooking. "Since you've managed to extract all the relevant details, how about you return the favor. Starting with his three buddies and anything else you might have gleaned while sitting here."

Dax and Mac came in and the front door slammed behind them, interrupting Lily.

"Hey, Gage." Dax crossed the room. "Hi, Lily. I'm surprised to see you here."

Mac snorted. "You're joking. There's a new case, and

Lily has been in it right from the start. I'll bet she beat Gage here this morning."

Lily grinned. "And Sharon too."

"Did I hear my name?" Peabody came around the corner. "About time you two showed up. We need to do one final sweep of the dining room before the ladies arrive. Gage wants to let the wedding prep get back underway."

Dax gave me a questioning look.

"Mac, why don't you and Peabody get started. I need to talk to Dax for a second."

Looking at Dax, Mac said, "I'll meet you in there."

Once they were out of hearing range, I looked to Dax. "I was going to talk to Mimi and Nikki's mom when they got here, but is there any way to cast a spell that would protect any evidence we might overlook now, so if there is something, it would be preserved?"

His brows knitted together. "Potentially, but I'll want to talk with Mimi first. Together we might be able to do something."

"Good, head down to the dining room. Lily and I are just finishing up another conversation."

He gave her a quick wink. "Good luck in the hot seat."

With a wave of her hand, she laughed. "This is easy. It used to be harder when he didn't know I was behind the scenes trying to solve puzzles for him."

My eyebrow hit my hairline. "What are you talking about? I don't recall you ever trying to solve any crimes before Flora's death."

She laughed. "Dax, can you believe he has no idea all the nights over dinner when he was telling me about the different goings-on in town that I wasn't problem solving things for him. He'd run down his day, and I would listen and then offer advice where it was needed. Back then, it seemed solving the mystery of cookie money stolen from William was the worst of our crimes in Pembroke Cove, but now things have gotten a bit dicer."

I smiled at the memory of Lily helping me to solve the cookie caper, where a couple of grade school kids stole money from William on a dare and it was Lily who figured it out. "That was around the time you adopted Milo too."

"Now the clues are knitting together." She clapped her hands together and grinned. "Good times, Detective."

"And now look. This is our sixth murder we're collaborating on." And it felt like the most natural thing to do. Some couples talked about the weather and what movie they're going to see next week. Lily and I write up clue boards and solve murders.

"Now, you were about to tell me the details of your conversation with Mr. Bailey's friends."

Her smile faded. "I don't think they were friends in the true sense of the word. As we were talking about John dying from hitting his head in the tub, not one of them seemed overly concerned except for where his boots were. The only other detail was John had been working with a local, and they don't know who it was. One odd thing, they said that any super important detail, he wrote down and stored it in his boot."

"That would explain why someone would want his boots."

Nodding, she said, "And the last time they saw John, he was wearing them. If we find the missing boot, we might just find an important clue as to why he was killed."

"Like a pirate treasure isn't enough reason?" I teased.

"Are you kidding? If the treasure was real at one time, it's long gone. For the record, we are not going in any caves or other freezing-cold places looking for clues." She winked, "I have other methods of finding lost treasure."

As a witch, she had many resources at her fingertips and now that she had a wand, her witchy world had expanded even more. I leaned forward. "I promise, no caves. At least until summer when maybe we should go looking for buried pirate treasure."

She groaned. "Well, don't tell Donnie White. He'll turn wherever we go into his next tourist destination."

"With that, I need to see him. I'll be back in a bit."

Chapter 10
Lily

An hour later, Gage came into the lounge at the Pembroke Cove B & B. He sat next to me, took my hand and pressed it to his lips. It was a sweet gesture and caused my heart to flutter. "Aunt Mimi and Iona are on their way, and Nikki is with them. With that much combined witch power in the dining room, we should be able to not just protect any remaining evidence, but keep it locked in time forever." When Gage didn't laugh, I tipped my head. "Not funny?"

His shoulders slumped like he was carrying the weight of the world on them. "This case has me baffled. No real evidence to point us in any direction as to who might be the killer. A vague reference to someone local helping them look for pirate treasure of all things."

I understood his frustration, and I was going to give him a pep talk to bolster his spirits. But an image in my head was like a negative being developed in a dark room, as photo paper sat in the developer and an image slowly began to appear. "We need to find the missing boot."

His brows knitted together. "What will that help? If there was a note inside, it will be long gone."

"Probably but there could be something else overlooked. Here's a thought. Do we even know if the one boot that was outside was John Bailey's? Have you checked to make sure it was his size?"

"When we searched his room yesterday, he had a pair of sneakers and slippers next to his bed, which were the same size as the boot we found. However, we didn't find any boots in the room. We found two more costumes, which I guess would be necessary if the other ones got dirty."

I sat up straight. "Any chance I can poke around his room?" It was hard to disguise the excitement in my voice. "I won't touch anything, just look, and you can be with me the entire time."

The lines on Gage's forehead deepened, and his gaze darted around the room. I knew that look. He was torn between knowing I might pick up on a clue that could have been overlooked by others, and he also knew me; I'd find a way in, one way or another. It would be easier and faster for both of us for him to agree.

He was taking far too long to mull over the idea. "You think on it, and after the ladies leave, we can go upstairs for a quick look around."

I wondered if he realized my word choice wasn't giving him an opportunity to say no later. "Donnie came through early this morning while I was reading my magazine."

That caught his full attention. "Did he share anything of interest?"

I flashed him my best *cat who lapped up the cream* smile. "He was shouting to Katherine who was in the kitchen. Telling her he needed to get back out there and strike it rich. Otherwise, she'd have to sell her family's precious legacy."

The corners on his mouth dipped. "Sounds like money issues to me."

I held up my hand. "When he noticed me, he got all nice and tried to backpedal on being rude to his wife. Apologizing that he hadn't meant what he said about selling anything, least of all the B & B. He was overtired from work and now with the murder, he was stressed, and it was bad for business long term."

A small grin graced his lips. "I'm sure you reassured him that you hadn't been paying attention."

"You know me so well, but then I took the opportunity to ask him what it's like trying to get a boat ready for the upcoming season. After all, he said he spent all day working on his vessel so it only makes sense."

"Please tell me he opened up and told you something important?"

I shook my head. "It's what he said directly, but he talked about his crew members hanging out with the guys from Boston. They were filling the locals' heads full of nonsense, like if they took these three days off, they could join forces and search for the trunks of treasure."

Now I had Gage's full attention. "The only downside is he didn't say if any of them took time off, but my guess is, it had to have been pretty tempting for his crew members. They keep working for basic wages on his boat when, if they got lucky and discovered the buried pirate treasure, they could probably buy their own pleasure boats and spend every day at sea, and in the cold months head to a warmer climate."

With a snort, he leaned back in the chair. "That would be an ideal life if you found the treasure. But there's nothing out there. Like we said before, it's been over three hundred years since Black Sam supposedly stashed a fortune somewhere along this coast. And whoever spun this new part of the legend was using it as a way to drum up tourism at the end of a long cold winter."

"We need to know how long this twist of these three days surrounding Saint Patrick's Day has been circulating. If it's just been in the last few years, then we must trace it back to the source."

"Lily, I admire your thought process, but that's like trying to figure out who said what at the start of a game of telephone."

"Between the new legend and the missing boot, we have two powerful clues. Don't overlook them, or worse dismiss them, thinking they're irrelevant. Until the case is solved, everything needs to be on the clue board."

I glanced at the door and got up from the chair. "Aunt Mimi is here."

He looked around, his face scrunched up, puzzled. "How do you know?"

I paused, unsure how I did know. "Well, she said she was on her way, so she must be here." I made a mental note to check my book or better yet, I could ask Milo. Could I have any untapped abilities like the tea reading skill?

He followed me to the front porch, and there was Nikki, her mother, and my aunt striding in our direction. The distinct set to their expressions meant they were coming to get the job done. Tomorrow was the wedding, and there was zero time to waste.

"Morning all," I called out.

Nikki ran lightly up the steps and gave me a tight squeeze. "Are we all set?"

I glanced around to make sure we were alone, that there

weren't any non-magical people lingering within hearing distance. "Almost." I kissed Aunt Mimi on the cheek and hugged Iona.

Gage stepped closer and said hello. "I'm going to let the reception take place in the room, but I was wondering if there's any kind of spell or incantation that you can perform which would hold any evidence of the crime in place, undisturbed. My officers believe we've got it covered but just in case."

Aunt Mimi gave him a thoughtful look. "Is Dax here?"

"He is, and I asked him the same question to which he believes there's potential. He said once you talked, between all of you, there could be a powerful spell." Gage looked at each of us. "So, it's possible?"

Aunt Mimi held her hands out, palms up as if channeling energy. She was a cosmic witch and drew her power from the moon and the stars. "My dear, everything is possible."

If I were to guess, she had prepared for whatever might be needed today under the moon last night. I looked at Iona, unsure what kind of a witch she was. Then I noticed the crystals hanging around her neck. She wrapped her hand around the pendant and closed her eyes momentarily. When she opened them and focused on me, she smiled. Her power washed over me like ocean waves crashing the shore at high tide, intense but not scary.

With confidence that welled up in me, I said, "Gage, not to worry. We've got this covered." I stepped back, and he opened the door as we entered the B & B single file.

"The dining room is down the hall straight ahead," he said.

"And who else is in the room?" Nikki asked.

"Sharon and Mac, along with Dax," I replied. "If we

need Dax with us, Gage could suggest that Sharon and Mac go back upstairs and take a final look or, even better, head back to the station."

"Lily's right. Give me a minute to talk with the team and you can get started with the overarching spell, and then the real fun will begin—cleaning up."

Nikki popped her hands on her hips. "Gage, we have four witches plus Dax if he cares to lend a hand; cleaning up is a snap." She demonstrated by clicking her third finger and thumb together, and then she grinned.

He shook his head. "I always forget that little detail." He glanced at the doorway. "Mimi, are you going to use magic to find the cutlery?"

"That will be the most expedient way. Do you object?"

He frowned as he stuck his hands in his coat pockets. "No. I think it's the best way to go about it at this point. I'm just not sure how I can explain to Peabody and Mac how I stumbled on the clue."

"We can figure that out once I have discovered the location. It would be helpful for Nate, if he didn't have to lug another box down from the attic."

"Can't you just wiggle your fingertips, and they'll appear? I've seen Nikki do that with a cake."

His question was innocent, but Aunt Mimi scowled. "Nate insists on doing some things his way and bringing items down from the attic is one of them."

I had seen that face many times, and it was never good. Before she went down that rabbit hole of why Nate should want to lean into her magic, I said, "Gage, do you want to talk with Sharon and Mac?"

He flashed me a grateful smile since he too had seen her get upset about things she couldn't control. It was nothing to do with magic since he had learned about Aunt Mimi at the same time I told him I was a witch. But my aunt was a formidable woman who liked things mostly her way. And Nate accepting her help with magic was one of those subjects.

"I'll check that the scene is clear." He stepped through the double glass doors, closing them behind him.

"Aunt Mimi, what about this spell to preserve evidence that might have been overlooked?"

Dax entered the hallway from the dining room and looked at the four of us. "Care to cast a few spells? A protection spell would be the most effective in this case to make sure nothing else happens. In addition, we can cast one to cleanse the room for the nuptials as well as maintain any evidence that might have been overlooked."

"The power of three spells combined into one." I nodded. "Sounds like a plan to me. We should wait until Gage and the others head upstairs." Nikki stood apart from us, and I pointed to the front door and gestured for her to follow me.

Once on the porch with the door firmly closed, I gave her a moment to tell me what was troubling her. After a very long and silent minute, I put my hands on her shoulders. "Spill it."

She looked into my eyes and without blinking, she said, "This is a sign that Steve and I shouldn't get married."

I wasn't sure if it was a good thing or not that she wasn't more upset as she spoke.

"What are you talking about? After we fix things up, it will be smooth sailing right on to the honeymoon."

Wringing her hands, she cried, "How can you say that? Your aunt's priceless cutlery is missing, broken heirloom dishes and a destroyed wedding dress that's in police custody. Oh, and don't forget a dead person found in the tub of the room that I was supposed to use. Everything comes in threes and with what's happened, I'm out of chances for anything else to go wrong."

Giving her a grin, I said, "That's four so it's already over the limit."

She groaned and turned away from me. "All that means is there are two more bad things to happen."

Nikki needed reassurance and I searched for a logical way to try and allay her fears. "Poor John Bailey wasn't connected to your wedding; therefore, all the bad things that could have happened for your special day are over and all is fixable. The dress has been replaced. Nate is bringing more dishes, and Mimi is going to find every last fork, spoon, and knife."

Without turning around, she continued to look at the empty street. "Then why did all this bad stuff happen in the dining room where I'm having my reception?"

I had a working theory and figured now was a good time to get it off my chest. "What if whoever killed Mr. Bailey was hoping by trashing the dining room, it would buy them time before he was discovered. I believe it was done after whatever happened upstairs. The perp panicked and when he or she came downstairs, they seized the opportunity as a distraction."

Nikki perched on the railing and gave me her full attention. "Do you really think that could be how it all played out?"

"I do. If you think about it in this light, what happened has more to do with misdirection."

Seeing a glimmer of her smile as she nodded gave me hope she was coming around.

"You're right." She threw her arms around me and held me tight. "This is why you're my best friend. Not only can you help me see the logic of things, but the way your mind works, you always figure out the puzzle. I'd bet money that your idea of how this happened is spot-on."

Laughing, I said, "Time will tell, but for now, we need to get back inside. There are a few spells to cast, and I think having an accomplished and a newbie witch on hand might help it along."

She looped her arm through mine. "When I'm back from my honeymoon, you and I are going down to Portland to have a spa weekend, and it's my treat."

"That's a plan, but you don't need to pay for me." Pulling open the door, I said, "The bride goes first."

Our steps were lighter on the way down the hall than when we had gone in the opposite direction. The doors to the dining room were standing open, and Aunt Mimi was in the middle of the room, her eyes narrowed and her hands on her hips. I noticed Gage and the others were gone. It was just Iona and Dax.

I stopped short, inside the door. "Aunt Mimi?"

"It's the darndest thing. I've tried the location spell, and I can't get an inkling on where the cutlery is. As if it's been cloaked by magic."

I looked at Dax and he shrugged his shoulders. "I tried too, but no luck."

Not speaking to anyone specifically, I said, "It's a good thing tomorrow is St. Patrick's Day. It would seem we could use a little leprechaun magic."

Nikki looked at me. "Or maybe that's what we're up against now."

Chapter 11
Lily

I snapped my mouth shut after saying, "Leprechauns aren't real."

Dax held up a finger. "Technically, you would have said the same about witches less than a year ago, so anything is possible."

He got me on that point. But for right now, we needed to get this room sorted out and ready for tomorrow. "True, any chance we can put that on the back burner for today?" Turning to my aunt, I said, "I'll call Regan to see if she can bring enough silverware for tomorrow. If not, I'll cross that bridge then."

"On the bright side, Nate will be here very soon with the dishes. Before he gets here, we need to cast our protection spell." She crooked a finger in Dax's direction, and he went to stand beside her. "You said you have an idea?"

He gestured for Iona, Nikki, and me to come closer and said, "I do. It's a triple spell that will provide protection for any evidence left behind and cleanse the room as well as protect all who will be here for the wedding."

My aunt nodded. "I wish we had one more witch to join

us to give us two times the power of three. But we can do this if we focus on bringing positive vibes to us and the space."

Dax smiled at each of us, and he gave Nikki a friendly wink. "Don't worry, this will work."

I liked how he had become a good friend to us in a relatively short period of time.

"I want us to repeat these words three times with our palms facing up.

Elements of the sun,
Elements of the moon,
Please come soon
Powers of the night and powers of the day
I call upon thee to protect this space and all who shall be here. For this I wish, so shall it be."

I looked at our little circle and we all nodded in agreement. Placing our hands with palms facing up and our fingertips touching each other's, we repeated Dax's words three times as requested, our voices blending together in a clear and decisive message. The room seemed to vibrate with energy, and I waited until Dax began to lower his hands before I followed suit. This was the first time I had been a part of a coven type cast, and if everyone else was feeling like me, well, we could tip the world on its axis right now or even better, get ready for a very important wedding.

Aunt Mimi beamed, Iona's eyes sparkled, and Nikki pulled Dax into a hug.

"I'm glad you decided to move to our small town and that we've become good friends. We couldn't have done this without you."

He disengaged from her hug and red flushed his cheeks

while his dark, almost black eyes morphed into velvet. "That's a nice thing to say, but you are all talented witches and wouldn't have needed me." He pointed to the door. "I'm going to check on the others unless there's something else I can help with?"

"Would you let Gage know we're done? And don't forget the rehearsal is at five. You're coming, right? Just in case we need to pump up the spell again."

"I'll fill him in and yes, I'll be here tonight." He hurried from the room as if the friendly feelings that had washed over him were a lot for him to handle.

I stared after him, wondering what his life was like before he came to Pembroke Cove on the fraud case. Had he been lonely living in a city away from other witches? Or did he have friends in DC and I was making assumptions?

"Earth to Lily." Nikki poked my upper arm.

I refocused on her. "Sorry about that. What were you saying?"

"Mom and Mimi said they had everything in hand here with the cleanup and suggested we bring the wedding cake over and get that set up. It will be one less thing for someone else to worry about after the rehearsal, and I'll feel better if I move it myself."

I stole a look at Aunt Mimi, and she nodded, agreeing that it was a good idea. "Great, we will take my car."

"Mom, while we're gone, can you figure out the best place to leave it overnight? I don't want anything happening to it."

Iona gave her a reassuring smile. "Don't worry, the room is protected, but I plan on protecting that cake with the strongest spell my wand can cast. It will look just as perfect tomorrow as it does today, and it will taste even better I'm sure."

I couldn't help but think, *From her lips to the goddess' ears*.

"Ready, Lily?" Nikki asked.

"Yes, soon to be Mrs. Jones."

"Oh, I do like how that sounds, but it's going to be Nikki Twing-Jones."

I looped my arm through hers. "Come on, Mrs. TJ. If we don't put a wiggle on it, we'll be late for your practice run."

As we walked through the doors, she said, "Like that would happen. If I had to, I'd slow down time."

I stopped walking and stared at her. "Can we do that?"

Laughing, she said, "In the words of your familiar, read your book."

I shook my head and muttered, "That should be engraved on my wand."

After the ladies were satisfied with the dining room, Iona and Nikki went back to her place to get ready for tonight and Mimi finagled lunch from Nate. Gage ran down the stairs and grinned. "Sorry the day has gotten away from me. Do you want to take a look at John Bailey's room before we go?"

Crossing my arms over my midsection, I was suddenly exhausted. "Is there anything left to see?"

"Nothing new, and since it's late and we still need to get to the rehearsal, I've sealed the room so you can look around day after tomorrow."

I knew it was for the best, but my shoulders dipped with the weight of disappointment resting heavy on them. I held out my hand. "You're right, Nikki and Steve have been through enough. I don't want to add any stress to them by being late for rehearsal."

He slipped an arm around my waist and pulled me close, and I giggled. "Ms. Michaels. Will you do me the honor of saving the first dance for me tomorrow?"

I looked at him through my lower lashes, going along with his spontaneous playful mood. "If you ask me."

"Consider yourself asked." He kissed me, and I felt my knees grow weak. Oh, how I was crazy for this man.

When I woke the next morning, the sun was peeking in the windows, and the sky was pink with the first blush of dawn. Milo was stretched across the other side of my bed. I rubbed his belly, and he opened one eye.

"Is there a reason you had to wake me up? I was having the best dream that you brought me a trout dinner." He smacked his little kitty lips and rolled on his back. "Any chance we can make that a reality in the very near future?"

"Potentially. But I wanted to ask if you've felt neglected the last couple of days. With preparations for the wedding and finding another dead body, I've been a little distracted. I hate the idea that I might have shortchanged you in the process."

Milo rolled over and sat back on his haunches. He regarded me carefully. "Are you really concerned or is there a punch line in there somewhere?"

I rubbed the top of his soft head between his ears. "Totally honest. We've gotten closer over the last few months, and I knew Nikki's wedding was going to take some time, but like I said, I just feel stretched thin, and you've gotten a raw deal."

"This isn't a permanent situation. We're going to go back to playfully sniping at each other, and I can bug you about reading the family book."

"Well, about that, I would prefer you find a new phrase. Even Nikki is saying it now—*Read the book.*" I put air quotes around those last three words.

"It is an effective statement. But why did Nikki mention you should read it?"

I plumped the pillows behind me and one for Milo too. "Yesterday, she was talking about slowing down time to get something done, and when I asked her if that was a thing, she said those three little words. And in the same tone you use."

He sniffed. "I say them with the utmost love and concern. I'm sure she couldn't possibly have done the same."

"You're not answering my question slash comment."

Milo did a great imitation of a downward facing dog yoga pose. "She already did." When he straightened up, he said, "Next topic."

I flashed him a side-eye. "How do you know I have one?"

Tipping his head, he said, "Murder, clue board in the kitchen, you added to it last night, and with that basic evidence, it's as yet unsolved. Which means Detective Cutie needs your brain cells to kick in and do the heavy lifting."

"Gage doesn't need me to do his job for him." I felt I needed to stick up for my boyfriend.

Milo walked to the edge of the bed and hopped down.

When he reached the door, he paused. "Doesn't he? You solved the last five with very little help from him." He swished his tail. "Now, since I happen to know there isn't trout in the refrigerator, what about opening a can of sardines? I noticed a can on the pantry shelf. Especially since you're going to be gone all day at the wedding festivities."

"How did you—" I waved a hand. "Forget it. I don't want to know how you saw inside a closed cabinet." Flinging back the blankets, I slid my feet into slippers and grabbed my bathrobe from the foot of the bed. I scooped him into my arms and rubbed his cashmere-soft head with my chin and gave him a quick nuzzle. "Just because I love you, sardines it is."

A t nine forty-five on the dot, I pulled into Nikki's driveway. We had hair appointments at Twisted Scissors at ten o'clock. I tooted my horn, and she opened the door and waved for me to come in. I hurried inside, realizing that with the dress being stored at her house after the recent disaster, she was going to have more than a shoulder bag to carry to the car.

"Happy wedding day," I sang as I entered her house.

"Thanks! I've had to pinch myself a couple of times since I wasn't sure Steve and I would ever make this walk down the aisle."

"Don't do that. You'll give yourself a bruise." I took the garment bag from her and picked up a small duffel bag. "What else do you need?"

She looked around the kitchen. "Another coffee?"

"You can have one as soon as your butt is in the hair-dresser's chair."

With a wide grin plastered across her face, she said, "Then I'm ready to go."

I stepped outside, and Nikki paused in the doorway before locking up. "The next time I walk into this house, I'll have a husband and be a wife."

Giving her the moment she needed to let the idea settle over her, I walked to the car and stowed the dress and duffel bag in the back before slipping behind the wheel. Even when changes were the best ever, the enormity should be respected. A minute later, she got in and wiped her cheeks.

She pointed to her face. "Happy tears."

Clasping her hand, I grinned. "Of course they are. You and Steve are going to have an amazing life and despite the bumps of the last few days, this is the happy ending—or should I say beginning—you both deserve."

With a smile as wide as the Atlantic Ocean, she said, "I couldn't have made it without you as my best friend." Her face took on a more somber expression. "But you have to promise me that you won't try and solve this murder. Leave it to Gage this time. We're going on our honeymoon tomorrow, and I couldn't bear it if anything happened to you because you decided to go off by yourself and investigate."

I looked out the windshield, understanding she had my safety at heart since she had become Holmes to my Sherlock after promising Gage I wouldn't go off by myself when I got a new idea. This time I couldn't promise anyone that I wouldn't try to discover the truth on my own.

She pressed my hand harder. "I can see that expression on your face, the one where you set your mouth in a determined line. You just went super sleuth on me."

I gripped the steering wheel, not about to tell her what she wanted me to say. "I hate that someone was responsible for a visitor to our little town not going back to his life. Let's just say it was an accident and they didn't mean for John to die. Why not call for help?" But I knew it wasn't an accident. A blow to the back of his body, breaking his neck, and then leaving him in the tub was despicable. However, I wasn't about to tell Nikki the truth, not on her special day.

"Promise me you'll be extra careful while I'm gone?"

I held up my pinky, and she wrapped hers around mine. It was something we had done forever. "Pinky promise, I'll be a super sleuth on steroids of caution." It was the best I could come up with even if it sounded cheesy.

She threw her arms around my neck in a half hug. "I love you, Lily Michaels, but if we don't get to the hair salon, I won't be able to slip into my beautiful bride mode for the wedding."

"Oh, Nikki, all the fancy hair and makeup will do is enhance what I already see, the most stunning bride ever."

Pushing all thoughts of the investigation aside, I turned the ignition key and laughed. "Buckle up, buttercup, and don't worry. I'll get you to the church on time."

Nikki and I came out of the pastor's office where she had gotten dressed. She decided after everything that had happened, she didn't want to do it at the B & B. I peeked through the large double doors from the church vestibule into the sanctuary. It seemed as though the entire town of Pembroke Cove had filled the pews. That was a slight exaggeration since in reality there were only fifty people on the guest list. Steve was standing with the minister at the altar and next to him was Gage. He was handsome, his long, lean frame filling out the gray tux perfectly. His hazel eyes locked on mine, and he gave me an appreciative smile as he pointed from my shoes to my hair.

The dark-green dress suited my chestnut-brown hair and sable eyes. Nikki had known what she was doing when she chose it for me. I gave him a wink as I closed the doors.

"Steve is waiting for you at the altar, and he looks so handsome." Nikki was beautiful in her mother's A-line gown in cream antique lace over a champagne silk lining. One of the bell sleeves held a tiny pocket big enough for the pale blue handkerchief I had tucked inside. The small elegant train brushed the floor, and it was absolute perfection on the bride.

"Does he look nervous?" she managed to eke out.

"It seems like you have enough jitters for the two of you." I placed the cascading bouquet of pale-pink roses tied with an emerald-green ribbon in her hand. "Are you ready for me to open those doors?"

"In just a second. I have something that must be said."

Her face was serious just like her tone of voice. "What is it?"

"You and Gage are good together. I know it took a long time for the two of you to tell the other how you felt, but don't let it be another fifteen years before you take the next step."

Why was she thinking of me on her wedding day?

She gestured to her dress and flowers. "I'm standing here ready to marry the love of my life, and I want you to experience the same joy. You and Gage belong together and not just solving the latest mystery in town. Promise me you'll think about setting a date?"

I kissed her cheek and said, "I promise."

Chapter 12
Gage

The reception was in full swing, and I was a happy man. There were no signs of mischief when we arrived. I had Lily in my arms as we glided around the dance floor. I kissed her temple and inhaled her sweet perfume that reminded me of a flower garden on a summer day. "You look stunning."

She eased her head back and looked into my eyes, causing my heart to constrict. "You said that at least three times already."

"But it's the truth and I want you to know how important you are to me, and I don't tell you enough how beautiful you are, inside and out."

She wiggled her left hand in my face. "You put a ring on my finger, so I have a wonderful reminder." She lightly kissed my lips and despite our engagement, she hadn't mentioned setting a date yet.

I wasn't sure if I was relived or anxious. "Does all of this make you want to start planning our wedding?"

"Nikki and Steve dated for years before he popped the question." She looked around the room and smiled. "As much as I'm looking forward to marrying you, I'm really enjoying being engaged. It took us so long to get to this point; do you mind that I'd like to savor what we have a bit longer?"

Holding her tight, I said, "We have a lifetime together and there's something to be said for living in the here and now."

I could feel her body stiffen, and I danced her around so I could see what she was looking at. "What's Donnie doing here?" I said it more to myself than to Lily as we moved sideways so we could both observe what was happening.

He crept along the outer wall and slipped out the back door. Lily glanced at me. "Are you as curious as I am?"

"Yes, but act casual. We don't want anyone to think you've gone into sleuth mode, and I've morphed into detective mode."

"Good point." She squeezed my hand. "Dance us toward the door, but keep smiling."

I loved how this woman's mind worked and did as she suggested. When we got to the edge of the dance floor, she said to me, but really for anyone who might be wondering what we were up to, "I could use a breath of fresh air."

I held out the crook of my arm, and she placed hers through it and propelled me forward. Under my breath, I reminded her to act normal.

She glanced over her shoulder before closing the door behind us. The exit door at the end of the hall gave off a sliver of sunshine at the threshold where it was propped open. This could explain how someone got in the building and took the boots from the dining room. Lily moved ahead of me while her hand slipped from mine.

"Lily," I whispered, but she waved me off like I was a fly buzzing around. She was on a mission.

Easing open the door, she stepped onto the stoop before pausing to look around the backyard. "Where did he go?"

I slipped off my jacket and placed it around her shoulders. She was going to get cold fast in her short-sleeved dress. Noticing light around the door of the shed, I pointed to it. "He must be inside."

"Why go through the reception when he could just walk around the building?"

A crash from inside echoed in the frigid air. She picked up the hem of her dress and raced down the steps with me right behind her, but she was quick, even in heels. The door burst open, and Donnie came flying out, landing on his backside in a pile of melting snow. Standing in the doorway was John Bailey's friends. Arthur was flexing his fingers and shaking his right hand. It didn't take a genius to see he was the one who punched Donnie.

"What's going on here?" Lily demanded.

I put out a hand to help Donnie up from the ground. His cheek and eye were already deep red from where a fist had connected with his face.

"Nothing." Donnie glared at the three men. "A misunderstanding."

Arthur studied his knuckles and grimaced. "No, this guy is a cheat, and so are the men who work for him. They gave us false information about the location of the gold, and after tomorrow, we have to wait another year before it will be easier to find."

Dylan jabbed his index finger against Donnie's chest. "Give us back John's map, or we'll make sure everyone knows you don't know diddly about searching for sunken ships."

I stepped between the men. "Threatening people is against the law."

Dylan looked at me with fire in his eyes. "He took a map from us—well, from John."

Lily focused her attention on him. "What map? And how do you know for sure?"

"John texted us. We have an active group chat when we're searching for Black Sam's gold. The morning he died, he sent us a text saying he'd found it. We all assumed he was talking about the map. But since the cops"—Dylan glared at me—"never asked us about it, we're guessing they don't have it."

"A treasure map?" Lily asked.

He groaned and Arthur said, "Yes. John was the research expert of our group, and he had become friendly with someone in town who had access to some old history books. They've been narrowing down the last known points of the pirate ship."

"Hasn't that been done before?"

Lily's question was innocent, but the dark looks that flashed over the men's faces were anything less than reasonable. "It's a valid question. Would you care to answer why this information was more accurate than what other people have been following?"

As if explaining to a child, Arthur said, "It's simple. John mentioned the local person's family went back generations and had old journals that had recently come to light. For a small fee, John was given access to the information."

Now it made sense. Someone had paid for new, and potentially false, information, but I wasn't about to say that out loud. "Did any of you read the journals or was that all John's doing?"

Dylan said, "John came up a day early to meet with his source. That's why he sent the text. We think he found an important clue which he would have put in his boot."

My guess is he stashed it in the boot that was missing. "Do you think this local person knew where he would hide important information?"

Shay Keegan shrugged. "Maybe? It depends on how friendly they got." He pointed to the other two guys. "He told us his secret place the first time we started talking about joining up and hunting for the gold."

As we talked, the hostility level ratcheted down. Donnie had been quietly standing with us, and I turned to him. "How did you get involved with the group?"

"I run a business that thrives on people like them. The superstition around only being able to find the gold during a three-day period is ludicrous. I wanted to set up a charter to take them on an exploration of the coastline, and when John and I talked, he agreed it was a good idea."

"When was that and did you argue with him?" I pressed the point that there were five men and others were more entwined in this case than I first thought.

"I bumped into him early yesterday morning when I was filling up my coffee mug. We haggled a bit over the cost, sure. Taking the boat out with a full crew is expensive, and he didn't want anyone other than this group on the boat, which means they'd bear the full cost for the day, maybe a few days."

Arthur said, "No guts, no glory, right?"

Lily said, "And you don't think spending money chasing pirate treasure is taking a huge financial risk?"

He shook his head. "Do you have any idea what that treasure is worth? If we find it, we'll be set for life as well as famous. In our world of treasure hunters, our reputations would be legendary."

She lifted her chin, and the glint in her eye showed her

annoyance. "John's death is connected to this treasure. Does it seem like it's worth pursuing now?"

I watched them closely to see if her question made a difference in their perspective. Shay's shoulders slumped. Arthur's face fell, but Dylan's expression remained neutral, and Donnie perked up. "Absolutely, it's worth going after. True hunters never give up on the chase." He gave each man a pointed look. "Isn't that right?"

Dylan took one step in Donnie's direction. His voice held an underlying threat as he said, "You're only saying that because you have the map."

"If I had it, don't you think I'd be on my boat headed to the location?" Donnie glanced at me. "Detective, help me out here."

"The law can't vouch for what you would or wouldn't do if you had possession of the map, but a word of warning, Donnie. If you do have it, it would be in your best interest to turn it over to me so that we can continue our investigation. Withholding evidence is a crime."

He held up his hands as if he were surrendering. "I swear on the title to my boat, I don't have it."

As much as I didn't want to believe him since it would be easier to solve this murder with this information, I sensed he was telling the truth.

Lily asked, "Do you think the text *Found It* was referring to the map, or could it be that John found the actual treasure with this local person's help?"

Shay shook his head. "I've known John for a long time, and there is no way he'd keep finding the actual treasure a secret. And we had been talking about the map, so it makes sense."

Lily glanced at me, and I knew what she was thinking; we must find the missing boot. But there wasn't any possibility the person would have left a slip of paper inside even if we did.

"Just one more thing." Lily moved so that she was only looking at Dylan, Arthur, and Shay. "The morning John died, I saw you on the street. You were leaving the B & B and you were very annoyed that John hadn't joined you. You weren't concerned enough to go look for him?"

Arthur said, "We knocked on his door on the way downstairs and heard him mumble that he'd meet up with us later."

Shay said, "Well, that's not what he actually said. It was *not now*. He sounded like he was in a foul mood, and I didn't want to start the day off like that. It was my suggestion we leave him, and he could find us later."

Dylan said, "He ran hot and cold on these trips. Like he'd get so pumped that we were on the trail again, and then he'd get depressed we were never going to find the gold. It wasn't unusual that he'd be in a bad mood, but typically it was at the end of a day, not in the morning."

"But if he texted he found it," Lily pressed again, "wouldn't he be in an upbeat mood, ready to forge ahead?"

Arthur nodded and tapped his chin, his expression growing thoughtful. "She's right. I hadn't thought about it like that. He should have been on fire."

Donnie said, "Can I go now? I need to get down to the marina. Keith needs my help. He's having an issue with the navigation system."

I gave him a nod. "Just as a reminder, Donnie, if you do come across something like a map that John had been referring to, let me know right away."

He grimaced and didn't bother to look at the other men standing there. "I got it; withholding evidence is a crime."

He stormed off, seeming to forget he had just had an altercation with them.

Arthur said, "Can we go too? Tomorrow is our last day to treasure hunt, and I am sick of wasting time."

Dylan and Shay echoed his sentiment. I had no reason to keep on asking questions. "We need to talk about all of this before you leave town."

"Yeah, sure," Shay said.

I reached for Lily's hand. Before we walked away, she turned and said, "Are you sure it was John's voice you heard coming from behind the door?"

My forward momentum stopped. The question had been so obvious, and I had been concentrating on the mini brawl and missed it. "Shay, any idea?"

He looked to Arthur and Dylan and back to me. "It never occurred to me, but maybe it wasn't."

Lily gave me a triumphant look, and she whispered, "After the wedding, we need to go back to my house. I need to look at the board."

Chapter 13
Lily

I kicked off my high heels the minute I walked into the kitchen and called to Milo. Gage was right behind me and shut the door.

My fur ball came trotting around the corner. "Where's the fire?"

Scooping him up, I hugged him close. "Everything is fine, but Gage and I need to add some clues to the board and before we do, I want to get your dinner."

He gave me a slow, lazy blink of his eyes. "You're thinking of me first?"

"How about a can of tuna?"

He quickly agreed and then tipped his head and gave me a quizzical kitty look. "Am I in trouble or did you mess up a spell?"

"Neither. I've been gone all day and part of the night and wanted to treat you." I set him on the chair and crossed the spacious kitchen to the pantry, pulling out the chalkboard and a can of the promised tuna.

Gage set up the easel-style chalkboard facing the table and while I broke the tuna up on the plate, he put the teakettle on. With a smile on my face, I hugged him from behind. "Thanks."

He placed a hand over my hand resting against his chest. "We both could use a pick-me-up. Any chance you have some cookies tucked away?"

Milo jumped to the floor and wove around my legs. "Detective Cutie can wait until after you feed me. Now that I've been teased with dinner, I'm ravenous."

I placed Milo's plate on the floor and opened the cabinet where I had stashed a tin. "They're not homemade, but you can't go wrong with shortbread." Moving around the kitchen on autopilot, I withdrew mugs from the cabinet and placed them with milk and sugar and the cookies on a tray. I couldn't help but think about discovering Donnie with John Bailey's friends. Was it as simple as it sounded, trying to shore up a charter trip? But there was more hostility than that.

"What's going on in your brain?"

Gage's comment made my thoughts stop twirling. "I'm trying to see if there is more to the relationship between Donnie White and the men from Boston. If they've been coming up here for a few years, at the same time of year, they had to have bumped into each other prior to this visit. If that's the case, then why talk about chartering a boat this time, or have they in the past and it wasn't mentioned?" I put the tray on the table and studied the sparse information on the board.

John Bailey, Boston, victim.
No boots
Bathtub – location of dress
Treasure hunter
Three friends seen arguing and then MIA during the day
One boot found – victim reportedly stores things in boots

Time of death 10-12- struck with pot
Donnie MIA all day
Missing cutlery, missing/damaged wedding dress
I picked up a piece of chalk and added:
Found it = map?
John said meet later, but was it his voice?
Donnie and his crew – cheaters – false information on location?
Local contact unknown – generations and journals

I took a step back. "What are we missing?" Looking at Gage, I said, "Besides the boot and why vandalize the dining room and dress?"

The kettle whistled, and he poured water over the infuser and the smell of mint permeated the air. Taking several deep breaths, I felt as if an idea was right in front of me but continued to just be wisps in the air.

"Didn't someone else mention the crew of *Donnie's Treasure* also had been talking with John and his friends?"

"Katherine said Donnie and his men were talking with Dylan, Shay, and Arthur but John wasn't with them, and that was around ten."

I could feel the smile grow on my face. "That's it." Adding the seven names and the word meeting next to it, another piece of the puzzle locked in place. "One of these men killed John Bailey. It fits. They were all in the same place at the same time, and it was around the time of death. Someone was in John's room, but what if he was already dead and the killer answered for him when Arthur knocked on the door. Or maybe it was Arthur who was inside."

Gage nodded as he began to follow my thread. "It sounded like the guys were together, though, so that would clear them."

"Unless they're covering for each other."

Milo rubbed against my leg. "Ms. Witch, for what it's worth, you are a far superior sleuth than your fiancé."

I didn't have the opportunity to respond before he trotted from the room. Gage watched him and then looked at me.

"Did Milo have something valuable to add?"

Gage knew I often talked things over with Milo, and he had a network of familiars in town who all compared notes on what has happened—the gossip network for familiars was how I thought of it.

"He just complimented us on starting to hone in on the killer." To avoid looking at Gage, I poured tea into our cups and said, "We should relax and talk this through again from the beginning. We're not any closer to figuring out why the cutlery is missing and how it can be someplace that Aunt Mimi can't find. Which of course suggests that magic is at play." I sipped my tea. "Do you think the magical beings Nikki mentioned that come around in spring include leprechauns?"

He cocked an eyebrow like I had just fallen off the gullible train. "No."

"Why not? She never said what they weren't, so it is possible."

"They're a myth from Ireland that wear a little tricorner hat and a green suit with boots and oversized buckles."

I snorted. "You're talking to a witch. We're in the same category and with a black pointed hat, riding a broomstick, and wearing a cloak."

He crossed his arms over his chest and leaned back. His eyes narrowed. "You have a point, but I still don't think they're in the same category. In addition, there is zero evidence they would exist in Maine if they are real."

I grew thoughtful. That was a true statement, but it was something I'd talk to Nikki about when she got home from her honeymoon. I needed more information regarding other paranormals who might saunter into town.

Pointing back to the chalkboard, I said, "Let's assume the trio was lying about hearing someone talking in John's room. He must have already been with the killer." I smacked the kitchen table with my hand. "One of those men killed their friend, and I'm positive they know where the mystery map is and maybe even the treasure. Which makes the motivation the desire to cut him out of his share."

"If they found the treasure, there would be more than enough to be split four ways. But if your theory is correct, why are they still in town? Wouldn't they have left if they'd actually found the treasure?"

Placing my hands over my face to ease the headache that was beginning behind my eyes. I groaned, "Why isn't this clear-cut of who done it? I feel like the other cases I helped you on had a more linear path to discover who it was." I dropped my hands and blinked.

Gage smiled. "That's because you were actively investigating from the first moment you found the bodies. This time you had a major distraction, so it gave the police time to do their job."

My eyebrows skyrocketed to my hairline. "Good point and now that I have more free time, I can help."

He handed me a shortbread cookie. "You don't need to jump in. The clue board is a huge help, just laying everything out logically clears my mind and helps me to focus."

I nibbled on the cookie. "What do you think happened? And who did it?"

Gage drained his teacup and got up from the table. "It's getting late."

My mouth gaped open. "Are you kidding? I've gone over all my ideas, and you won't even give me a hint what direction you're leaning toward?"

He pulled me up from my chair and wrapped his arms around me, providing me a cocoon-like hug. "Five times we've talked in detail about what I thought, and five times you've come close to getting seriously hurt or worse. I can't in good conscience tell you what I'm thinking because you'll go off on your own tracking down clues."

I pulled out of his embrace and looked into his hazel eyes. "I have a few aces up my sleeve that keep me safe." To my ears, I sounded like a petulant child, but I was tired, had a headache, and I was annoyed that this murder had cost my aunt a family heirloom.

He pressed a sweet kiss to my lips. "I wasn't going to tell you this, but I talked with Peabody and Mac earlier today. We're close to arresting someone, so there isn't any need for you to follow up on the clues."

"There's still the issue of Aunt Mimi's cutlery. I intend on helping her track it down."

"I wouldn't expect anything less, but I think the vandalization of the dining room, the missing wedding dress, and cutlery don't have a connection to the murder. It was coincidence that it happened at the same time."

I nodded but that wasn't my idea; it was a diversion tactic. Since we didn't share the same thought process, I wasn't going to argue the point. Standing there, I realized I had to plan for tomorrow. There were people to talk with and threads to tug and see what unraveled. I needed to check in with Aunt Mimi about who could have strong enough magic to put up a block that even she couldn't penetrate. Not being boastful but my aunt was rumored to be the most powerful witch within the state of Maine.

Forcing myself to yawn, I said, "You're right. It's been a busy day, and we should get some rest. Maybe you could come by the bookstore for lunch."

"It's a date." He kissed me again, and I felt my toes curl. "I'll bring lunch."

"I'm already looking forward to it." I opened the kitchen door and watched him get into his truck. With a light toot on the horn, he drove in the direction of his house. I locked the door and with a wave of my hand, the kitchen table was cleaned, and the dishes were in the sink. I'd deal with them in the morning. Hurrying down the hall, I poked my head into the spare bedroom which was my home office. "Milo, how would you like to go with me tomorrow while I talk to a man about a charter?"

He lifted his head and then dropped it back onto a chair pillow. "I'll skip it, but if you're going to the marina, you might want to pick up some fish for dinner. It's been over a week since you made us a lovely seafood feast."

I popped my hands on my hips. "Milo. Do you only ever think about your next meal?"

He eased to a sitting position. "In my defense, I wasn't suggesting you get it for my breakfast. I can suffer through with a can of regular cat food, but you're going to want to talk over what you learn, so it will make it easier watching you plod through clues with a tasty piece of cod."

I threw my hands up. "I'll see what I can do, but you're going to owe me big-time on this one."

"Does it help that you have my undying thanks?"

Without answering him, I started down the hall to my bedroom. Calling over my shoulder, I said, "I'll let you know when I get home tomorrow night." A soft thud of Milo jumping down from the chair and the padding of kitty paws following me down the hall was comforting. I kept a smile in check, knowing he wanted to be with me. No matter what the fur ball said, he had my back.

Milo hopped up on the bed and asked, "What's your plan for tomorrow?"

I grinned and sat down next to him. "I'm glad you asked."

"Before you tell me, does Gage know what you're up to?"

"Nope, and as far as I'm concerned, what he doesn't know won't get him upset. Besides, when I go to talk to Donnie, it will be in broad daylight with other people around." I failed to mention that I was going to talk to the crew members too. Someone might have insight into why there was bad blood between Donnie and John Bailey.

A tiny niggle of worry crept up my spine. Usually, when I went off asking questions, Nikki was with me. But I pushed that aside. I couldn't wait for her to get back in a week since after tomorrow, the treasure hunters would be gone and with it my chance to help Gage close the case.

With a deep kitty growl, he said, "I don't like how that sounds. Maybe you should ask Gage to go with you."

Frowning, I said, "Please tell me you're joking. He would never willingly allow me to talk to a major suspect. He's always afraid I'll get hurt."

"Or worse."

Milo didn't need to point out I got myself into tough situations, but I also wiggled myself out too. "I'll be fine."

"What about your buddy, Dax? I'll bet he'd go with you if you asked."

Shaking my head, I groaned. "He's on the force too. Besides, I don't think Donnie will be as willing to talk with him around. It's going to be hard enough to get him to open up to me." I got up from the bed and turned back the covers.

"How about if I ask Nate to be at the marina around the time I plan to bump into Donnie. I can even say I was looking for Nate."

"It's not a bad idea." He gave me a thoughtful gaze. "How about we review the spells you've mastered as a refresher in case you need to use one."

I couldn't help but laugh. "Always the teacher." I rattled off the list of newly acquired skills, from lighting a candle with a simple breath, to finding lost objects, making something small vanish, and of course the most important, protection spells. Snapping my fingers, I smiled. "And let's not forget I can unlock doors." That was a skill that had come in handy when we were solving the case at Halloween. I had been able to get into the grange hall and do a little after-hours sleuthing, even though Gage had changed the locks. It was one of my finer accomplishments.

Milo picked his way over the mound of blankets, and after turning around three times, he settled on the extra pillow. "And you have the summoning spell so if you need help, tap into that."

I knelt on the bed and scooped him to my chest. "I promise to use any and all of my spells when needed." I kissed the top of his head and gently placed him back on the pillow. "Good night, Milo."

"Good night, my dear witch."

Chapter 14
Lily

The next morning the wind whipped the collar of my jacket away from my neck, exposing me to the frigid Maine air. I hurried across the parking lot and into the building marked White. I wondered where Nate was since he had agreed to meet me here, but I didn't want to hang around outside and make it look like I was waiting for someone in case I was being watched.

"Hello," I called out to what seemed to be an empty warehouse except for the large boat with the lettering on the back, *Donnie's Treasure.* From what Donnie had said to Gage, he had been here working on the boat with his crew. I walked deeper into the warehouse toward what I thought could be an office. The door was ajar, and a sliver of light spilled out. I called again, "Hello?"

The sounds of raised voices drifted my way, and it propelled me forward. Pausing in the shadow of the boat, I heard a male voice say, "This has gotten out of hand." I longed to know who said that and who he was talking to.

"I know, but now what are we going to do?" The other man's voice was clear without a trace of frustration or anger.

He was cool as a cucumber so that had to be the mastermind behind whatever it was they were talking about.

I took a step closer to the office. Oblivious to everything around me, I was intent on eavesdropping when suddenly a large hand grabbed my arm and whirled me around. My heart thundered in my chest. "Donnie." I forced a smile to my face. "I stopped by to talk with you for a moment."

He growled as his eyes narrowed. "Then what are you doing lurking outside the office. Hoping to get some dirt on me that you can share with your boyfriend?"

"Not at all. I was hoping to talk with you about the men from Boston who are staying at the inn." I wasn't about to confess that I was hoping he'd overshare and tell me what really happened the day John Bailey died and where he was since I surmised he wasn't telling his wife the complete truth. But, had he been the one to get into an altercation with the victim and spent the balance of the day lying low in hopes to keep off Gage's radar?

He eyed me with suspicion. "Then why are you out here loitering instead of entering the office?"

I pointed to the door. "It sounded like a couple of people were arguing so I thought it prudent to let them finish."

"Oh?" He turned to look in the direction of the office, but it seemed the argument had died down and there was nothing left for me to hear. With a sweep of his arm, he said, "Come on in then, since there's no reason to avoid the men."

I wasn't keen on having anyone know that I had over-heard anything, but I didn't have a choice but to walk ahead of Donnie. Despite the cold sweat slipping down my back, I reminded myself I was a witch. I could handle this situation. I winced as Donnie closed the door behind us.

The office was surprisingly tidy. There was a large desk

and worktable with a part from a boat, covered in grease, in some stage of either being assembled or disassembled. A stack of rags was also grease-laden next to the part. Hutch was sitting on a stool at the worktable—we had gone to school together. Keith was wiping his hands on a rag, and I recognized Jock from around town. Keith was a transplant from somewhere upstate. I recognized them all, but I hadn't realized they all worked for Donnie, or maybe they were just friends hanging out.

Keith stared at me. "Are you lost, Lily?" There was no mistaking the hostility in his voice.

I looked from him to Jock and Hutch. "No, but I had wanted to talk to Donnie about something."

Donnie sank to an old wooden desk chair and tipped back. "Anything you want to ask me, can be said in front of them."

Like a merry band of pirates flashed through my mind. Hutch stood up and offered me his stool next to the bench. I shook my head. "I'm fine to stand, but thank you."

"What did you want to know?" Donnie's glare hadn't been replaced by a friendlier look.

My stomach clenched. I took a few deep breaths and thought about what I needed to know. "Right. I was thinking about yesterday, when you had the altercation with the treasure hunters."

Keith sat up in his chair. "What's she talking about, Skipper?"

Donnie waved his hand. "It's nothing."

I tipped my head. He was trying to downplay what happened. That was interesting. "Why would they think that you had a map to the legendary treasure of Black Sam?"

"You need to ask them, not me." He looked at the floor and then to Hutch. "You know anything about some map?"

"Nope. Not me." He glanced my way. "We get a lot of those types when the charter's running. Looking for an easy way to find that treasure and then accusing us of holding out on them."

That sounded like what Arthur and his friends had accused Donnie of doing. Self-preservation kept me from pointing that out. "So that's common in this business?"

He nodded. "You have no idea the nutjobs we get. Some people understand this job is like looking for a needle in a haystack. I think they do it more for the thrill of the hunt and if they find something, that's a bonus. Treasure hunting is a passion, not a real way to riches. You're better off playing the lottery."

"Hutch, if that's the case, why do it?"

He snorted. "I'm happy to drum up business and be aboard the boat, help them in and out of their scuba gear. But, as far as really finding something in the frigid waters of the Atlantic, that's not for me."

Jock was nodding as Hutch explained his position. "Same here. If someday a group actually found something more than trash at the bottom of the ocean, I'd be thrilled. Besides, there's a clause in the charter contract that each member of the crew gets a small percentage of the find."

I glanced to Keith and then Donnie. "Is that standard for all treasure hunters?"

Keith shrugged. "Who knows. Most businesses don't share their contracts with the competition."

That made sense. I wouldn't give a new bookstore all my secrets I'd learned over the years and from working with Aunt Mimi. "Keith, why do you think these men are so quick to point a finger at Donnie?"

He crossed his arms over his rather large belly. "Their buddy's dead and sounds like he took some information with him to the great Davey Jones's locker in the sky. I'll bet they're kicking themselves for not asking him more questions before leaving the inn that day, figuring they'd catch up later."

Donnie stood. "We've got work to do."

There was no mistaking that he was anxious for me to leave. "One more question. The men were planning on chartering *Donnie's Treasure* this summer. Will you take them out?"

"Money is money. If they still want to go, then we'll take them." Donnie didn't look at the men since it was his boat and all decisions were his.

I nodded to the project on the bench. "I'll let you get back to whatever it was you were doing."

As I walked out the door, I slowed my steps. "Keith, what did you mean when you said they must be kicking themselves. How did you know they hadn't had a conversation?"

He leaped up from the chair with such force it flew back and hit the wall, his fists balled at his sides. "Are you accusing me of something?"

"Of course not, I thought it was a curious comment, that's all." I arched a brow and took a step closer to the door while my fingers itched to throw up the protection spell.

The door banged open, and Nate filled the doorway with the bulk of his frame. "Lily, what are you doing down here?"

I eased to his side. "I came down to see if you'd like to go shopping with me for a gift for Aunt Mimi, and while I was here, I popped in to see Donnie. After getting sucker punched yesterday, I wanted to make sure he was all right."

Hutch said, "Who punched you?"

Donnie waved a hand. "Not important." He nodded at Nate. "Good to see you both. Take care walking through the warehouse."

That was effectively a dismissal and was there also an implied threat? I put a hand on Nate's arm. I still needed an answer from Keith.

"I believe you were about to tell me why you thought Mr. Bailey's friends might be upset."

Beet-red color flushed his face, from the base of his neck to his hairline. "Isn't it obvious?"

I gave him a sweet smile despite my insides quaking. "Not to me."

He rolled his eyes. "Plain and simple. They left the inn without him and later he was found dead."

He was right and I noticed he was flexing his fists as if trying to get cramps out of them. "Of course." I forced a friendly smile to my face as I looked at each man before I walked out with Nate. Was it too much to hope one of them would have a telltale sign that they weren't being completely honest? "Have a good rest of your day, gentlemen." Dang, that sounded lame, but it was the only thing I could think that would gracefully get me out of there without accusing any of them of something more.

Nate closed the door behind us and grabbed my hand, tugging me in the direction of the illuminated Exit sign. Once outside, he stopped and turned to me. "Lily, what were you thinking going in there by yourself?" He held up his hand to stop what he knew was coming next. "I know you can handle yourself, but other than Donnie, those men have hot tempers, and I wouldn't want to be in a room alone with them. They're not like most crews in Pembroke Cove. These guys are borderline dangerous."

I adjusted my shoulder bag as my heart rate became more regular. "How come no one has ever talked about them before now? Are they really dangerous?"

"People around the marina talk about how those three are always spoiling for a fight. They poach charters with promises of finding the gold. They even do some fishing charters promising the best day on the water."

Now I was confused. I never knew there was a downside to the charter business. "Do you think one of them could have killed poor John Bailey?"

He shrugged. "I'm not sure, but please don't go back to that warehouse by yourself. I don't trust any of them and that includes Donnie White."

Looking back over my shoulder, I nodded. "I won't. But I did glean some information for my clue board. As much as they didn't say anything about John's death, they gave me a lot about their business ethics, or really lack of."

Nate shook his head. "I know what that sparkly look in your eyes means too; you're ready to follow up on a new clue."

I grinned. "There are three men dressed as leprechauns that have some explaining to do, but at least this time I can meet them on neutral ground and be prepared with my questions."

He kissed my cheek in a sweet uncle kind of way. "Be careful, and if you need me, just give me a call. I'm always happy to look after my favorite, and recently inherited, niece."

"See what being married to Aunt Mimi gave you?" I held up my hands, palms toward the sky, and chuckled.

He tweaked my nose like I was a little girl, and we both laughed.

"Thanks for coming down, Nate, and please, don't tell

Aunt Mimi I went off half-cocked and got these guys all riled up. I was down here, but I don't want her to worry about me."

"She worries about you even if she doesn't know what you are up to. It's your nature to poke around and hers to worry. I like to think of the two of you as the yin and yang." He pointed to my blue and white Mini Coop. "I'll wait until you drive off. Not that I think that crew will bother you again, but call me the overprotective uncle."

I gave him a quick hug. "I appreciate you looking out for me." A shiver raced down my spine, and I turned to look back at the warehouse. I had the uncomfortable feeling we were being watched. "You might want to follow me. After all, we are supposed to be shopping for your bride."

He nodded. "Good point. I'll be right behind you, and once we hit the main road, you can head for home."

"Actually, I'm going to run to the bookstore. There are a couple of things I want to look up about our notorious pirate, Black Sam. The books on local history are about to come in handy."

Nate and I crossed the lot and got into our cars. With a jaunty wave, I went west, and he went north. A few moments later I parked in front of the Cozy Nook Bookstore and hurried to the door. With a sleight of a magical hand, I unlocked it and went inside. Oh, how I wish I had known years ago that I was a witch. So many things in life would have been simpler.

I locked the door behind me and flicked on the overhead light with a whisper of a spell. *Lights on, lights off, the opposite of what is will be.* That went very well. Pleased that my magic was definitely getting stronger, I shrugged off my coat and dropped my shoulder bag in one of the wingback chairs where I often enjoyed a cup of coffee.

Crossing the room to a small bookcase that held local authors who wrote nonfiction, I scanned the shelves but found nothing on pirates. I could do a location spell, but half the fun of a bookstore was the poking around, even if it was your own store, and with all the inventory, it was easy to lose track of an obscure title or two.

I strolled up and down a few aisles, straightening things as I went, letting my mind wander. I needed to talk with John Bailey's friends before the end of today. Tomorrow they'd be leaving town.

My eye caught sight of a book with bold red lettering on the spine, and I withdrew it from the shelf. *Pirates of North America, The Truth Behind the Legend.*

The clock inside the store struck the hour, and if I hurried, I could get back to the B & B before the treasure hunters had a chance to go inside, maybe.

I pulled on my coat, opened the door, and ran directly into Gage.

"And where are you off to in such a hurry?" he asked.

Chapter 15
Gage

I placed my hands on Lily's shoulder to steady her as she bounced off my chest. If she looked me in the eye, I would know if she was telling me the whole truth. If her eyes focused on my nose, it was a half-truth.

"Gage. I wasn't expecting to literally bump into you." She tipped her head to the side and gave me her practiced, sweet and innocent look.

I swear if she was a *batting her eyelashes* kind of girl, she would have done that too, but she was up to something. On that point, I was sure. "I was surprised to see your car out front. I thought you were going to take the day and recover from the wedding festivities. A lot has been going on over the last few weeks as you helped Nikki get ready."

She still hadn't moved either inside or out of the store. Was she weighing her options? I nodded to the door. "Why don't we go in and talk about what you've been up to today?"

Her eyes narrowed slightly and that was her tell. She had been poking around in the investigation. "Or we could wander over to the Sweet Spot and get a coffee. Maybe William made your favorite today."

"A cinnamon pecan roll would hit the spot, and a caffeine jolt is always in order. If you want to go over and get it, I'll wait for you here."

Tricky witch. "Let's go together. We haven't spent a lot of time just chatting, and I've missed this kind of stuff." It was the truth. I had missed just being with Lily, having coffee and talking about anything and everything. It was just one of the reasons I fell in love with her, the ease between us.

Glancing at her car and then across the town green to the bakery, she said, "I'll just leave the lights on for us."

She slipped her hand in mine as we crossed the street and then wandered down the stone lane that bisected the green into several walking paths. "Nice weather."

I held back a chuckle. "It is. The sun feels warm even though there is still a winter nip in the air." Two could play this casual conversation game.

"How's Brutus?"

"He's good. Just a big lug of love. All he does is sleep during the day while I'm at work."

She glanced at me. "You could bring him over to the shop a few days a week. He and Milo are becoming buddies, and that way he won't get lonely when you're at work."

"That's a great idea, but what about your customers? He's a big dog and people might be nervous around him." I liked the idea of giving him other options for when I was working. In addition, being with Lily and Milo was perfect as one of these days, we'd be a family, all living together under one roof.

Grinning, she said, "Are you kidding? Everyone will

love him, and if I think someone is nervous, I'll ask him to lie down in his bed, and it will be fine. He's such a sweet boy."

We reached the bakery, and I pulled open the door. Smells of yeasty goodness and sugar teased my senses and set my mouth to watering. It was like this every time I came in here, and you'd think after all these years I would have become immune, but I guessed that was part of the magic. "Hi, William," I called out even though the older gentleman wasn't directly behind the counter.

"Be right there," was the muffled answer.

I pointed to the case. "Lily, we're in luck." Sitting in the case was a metal baking tray full of cinnamon buns. On the top of the icing was a sprinkling of chopped pecans.

"I'll get our coffees."

She moved to the coffee bar and set about doing her thing while I looked out the front window. Donnie White's truck cruised slowly past the bookstore, creeping along as if trying to see who was inside.

I moved closer to the window, but I was distracted when William said, "Gage, what can I get for you and Lily today?"

"As if you need to ask with that fresh tray of my girl's favorites in the case. We'll take four, but can you package them in boxes of two? One for now and one for later." I turned back to the window, but the truck was gone. At this time of day, shouldn't Donnie be at the marina? And if what he said was the truth about the day of the murder, he had a boat to repair to be ready for a launch date sometime in early April.

"Here you go, Gage." William placed two boxes in a white paper bag and punched a few keys on the cash register. Before I could get my wallet out, Lily handed him cash and gave me the bag.

"Well, hello to you too, Lily," he joked.

She placed a hand over his and smiled. "I'm sorry, William, but we need to get back to the store. I was in the middle of something when Gage lured me away with the promise of a tempting treat."

He chuckled. "Go on, you two. Enjoy the rest of your morning." His eyes grew misty. "I remember what it was like with my sweet Lulu. The simple moments are the ones I miss the most." He dabbed his eyes with the edge of his apron.

Lily went around the corner of the counter and folded the older man into an all-encompassing hug. "We should get back on track with our monthly dinners. What do you think about next week? I'll cook."

He gave her a squeeze before releasing her. "I'd like that, and I'll bring dessert."

He looked at me, and I said, "Together, Lily and I will whip up a delicious meal."

She said, "Hey, I know what you're really saying. I might not be a great cook, but we wouldn't starve." And then she laughed. "Who am I kidding? If Gage didn't help in the kitchen, what he'd need to bring was takeout."

And there was another one of Lily's qualities that I loved, her ability to be comfortable with things that weren't her strong suit. She had so much talent in so many ways, how could she be good at it all?

I slipped my arm around her shoulders and kissed her cheek. "That's why we make a great couple. The yin and the yang."

She gave me a sharp look but didn't say what was on her mind. Instead, she smiled again at William. "Dinner on Wednesday?"

He tapped his temple. "You're on my busy social calendar."

Lily fluttered her fingers in his direction right after she pulled open the door without waiting for me to do it. "Bye, William, and we're already looking forward to dinner."

"Me too," he called after us as I closed the door.

Before we had taken ten steps, Lily said, "Have you been talking to Nate today?"

Where had that question come from? "No, was I supposed to?"

She stopped walking and looked me directly in the eye. I didn't blink, not sure what she might say or do next.

"Is that the truth?"

"I have never, nor would I ever, lie to you. I might not tell you something if it's confidential for my job, but overall, our relationship is based on complete honesty. What's upset you."

"Something Nate said, but it's fine. You two must think alike." Pausing for another moment, her face relaxed, and she started walking again. "I'm glad William had the buns today."

Before we reached the sidewalk, I saw Donnie White's truck cruising down the street again, but this time whoever was behind the wheel adjusted the hat on his head lower, wore dark glasses, and sped up when he saw us. I couldn't swear it was Donnie if I'd been asked.

"What was he doing here? He should still be at the marina." Lily watched as the truck turned the corner at town hall.

That tone in her voice set off the warning bell in my head. What had she been up to earlier? As soon as we were sipping coffee, it was time for me to find out. With a killer on the loose and Nikki not around to go with her as she tracked down clues, that meant she was probably off doing it on her own. My blood chilled in my veins. I hadn't thought she would have dived into the case since I was close to an arrest, but inwardly, I knew the challenge would be hard to resist. She loved solving any kind of puzzle which included the cutlery, and murder was the most captivating for sure. The layers of why would always fascinate her.

We had crossed the street, and I noticed Milo was sitting in the bookstore window, his gaze locked on us. It was too bad I couldn't talk to him since Milo was sure to know what Lily had been up to.

We got settled in our usual wingback chairs near the front of the store. It had a view of the street while still being cozy. I handed her the box, and she handed me a coffee cup with the sippy part tucked back.

I sipped the dark roast and said, "I wonder if Donnie White had gone back to the inn for something, maybe to help clean up from the wedding reception."

She snorted. "He's the type of guy who's hands off when it comes to cleaning. The B & B is strictly Katherine's domain and his is the marina."

"Katherine does a great job. From what I've learned, her business is strong no matter what he implied the other day."

"It's good you checked into it. I would guess a lot of repeat guests is the key to her success." She nibbled on a bun with a contented sigh.

"I was impressed with how clean and tidy it was. With people coming and going, I guessed it wouldn't look as pristine." I wasn't sure where my comments would lead, but with any luck I'd unearth whatever she was hiding since she avoided the questions of where she was going when I arrived.

"It must run in the family. Donnie's office is just as tidy even with work in progress."

I cocked a brow and gave her a long look before asking, "How would you know about his office?"

She didn't look at me but instead picked at the chopped nuts on her bun. "Um. It's just an educated guess based on how they live. Did you notice if his clothes were greasy when he got to the B & B on the day of the murder?"

"Now that you mention it, I don't think so. I didn't see any dirt on his hoodie."

Her eyes grew wide. "Dang, that just fell into place. I hadn't even realized that until this very moment."

"Why would you think he should have grease on his clothes?"

She squirmed in her chair. "Because when I was at the marina this morning and in Donnie's office, the space itself was tidy, but there was a greasy engine part and rags on a worktable. If he had been working on that part, like he said, there is no way he wouldn't have gotten grease on his clothes."

Now the slow drive-by made more sense. She had riled someone up, and since I couldn't be sure it was Donnie, I wasn't going to dwell on it at the moment. "Did you go down there alone?"

She blew out a breath which caused her bangs to flutter. "Yes. It's not like I could call you up and say, want to go chat up Donnie at the marina?"

"Well, you could have."

"Um. No. It wouldn't have gotten me the answers I was looking for."

I held my temper in check since it was more about Lily's safety than her actually trying to solve the murder. "And did you?"

A gleam lit up her eyes. "I think Donnie and his crew aren't very ethical when it comes to their business, but he never told the guys about his run-in with Arthur, Shay, and Dylan. And"—she held up her pointer finger—"Keith mentioned that it was too bad John's friends hadn't talked to him before they left that morning. How did he know they didn't?" She snapped her fingers. "That's not all, Donnie said if the three guys still want to charter his boat and search for the treasure, he'd take them."

I had to admit this was interesting, and it indicated that possibly the eight men had been in cahoots about something. But as far as I was concerned, it was nothing more than a charter trip. "Donnie is a businessman. If people want to pay him to go on a wild goose chase, isn't that his job?"

"Yes, and Hutch and Jock said something to that same point that even if you don't believe the gold is real, there isn't harm in providing a service to help people follow their dream."

"Exactly."

She frowned. "What about Keith's comment?"

"It's a logical assumption that they didn't talk since Bailey remained behind and his friends left."

Lily jumped to her feet. "Then one of them is the killer. We have to stop them before they leave town." She put her coffee cup down and grabbed her handbag. "Come on. We need to get to the B & B."

I continued to sit where I was, casually sipping my coffee. That's where she had been headed when I arrived— to talk to my three primary suspects. "They won't be back to the inn for another couple of hours. I've already checked with Katherine. All of their stuff is in their rooms, and they told her to expect them for dinner tonight, and they plan on checking out in the morning."

Lily leaned against the chair. "Are you sure or are you just saying that to keep me from going over there?"

"Are you kidding? You're hot on the trail, and I wouldn't dream of stopping you. However, I do want to slow you down just a little bit."

She gave me a side-eye. "And?"

The front door to the bookstore opened, and Dax walked in. I gave him a smile. "Lily, meet your new Nikki."

Her mouth fell open, and she said, "You can't be serious. He's a cop."

I nodded. "True, but he's new, and he has the one skill that I don't. He's a witch and can help you get out of a tight spot if needed." Getting up from the chair, I kissed her lips. "If you insist on following this puzzle until the end, promise me you'll let Dax be your substitute Holmes."

She looked from me to Dax. "Just to be crystal clear, if you're coming with me, you're not a cop. You're just a friend."

Dax grinned. "Does this mean I need to learn how to bake and keep you supplied in cookies?"

Lily shook her head. "I have a feeling this isn't going to be as easy as it would be with Nikki." She gave him the once-over, looking at his suit coat and dark jeans. "You're going to need to lose the jacket and look more like you blend in. You're still dressing like a federal agent from the city."

He chuckled. "You can take the man out of the city, but you—"

Laughing, she said, "I'm going to stop you right there. Since you aren't wearing the last coat we bought, maybe there's something more suitable at Bee Bee's Boutique. She carries men's clothes too." She plopped down in her chair.

"But first, I'm going to finish my coffee and cinnamon pecan bun. I think shopping with you will require all my strength since the only color you seem to like is black."

Dax sat across from us in his usual chair. "Black is my color."

Lily winked at him. "As my sidekick, things are going to change, my friend."

I exhaled. Lily would be safe with Dax, but would he survive shopping? I smothered a grin. "Just be careful out there, you two."

She winked. "Don't worry. I'll take care of Dax and return him to the force the same way he is now—well, except with a better wardrobe."

Dax laughed. "That depends on who you ask."

She balled up a paper napkin and threw it at him. "Trust me. You'll see."

Chapter 16
Lily

After I had taken Dax on a quick trip to the boutique, he had a stylish new coat and a few wool sweaters in muted colors along with two pairs of jeans, one dark wash and the other black. To be honest, I loved the excuse of him being my shadow to spruce him up a bit more. He was a handsome guy, and if he was going to stay in town, he needed to date. Dressing like a federal officer wasn't going to be good for his romantic life.

We strolled back to his car to drop off the shopping bags. The day had turned to our advantage; the sun was warming up, and the breeze had died down. "Now, Dax, when we stop by the B & B, we're going to have tea with Katherine, and this will give us a good vantage point of the front entrance. When Shay, Arthur, and Dylan show up, we'll invite them to join us."

"And what if they say they're short on time?"

"I'm prepared with questions about Black Sam's treasure. I read about it online, and today while you were trying on clothes, I skimmed a book I had in the shop." I withdrew it from my bag and handed it to him. "You might want to do the same before tea."

He took the book and held it up. "Do you think this is the key to discovering what motivates people to seek the treasure?"

Leaning against his car, I said, "I get why people do, the adrenaline of finding a cache of gold that had been stashed by a pirate. But have you considered why there are only four people in town looking for the treasure at this time of year, and they come year after year? So, who's feeding them misinformation that this is the time to find the treasure and why now? Treasure hunters could be seduced into believing it was at Easter or Ground Hog Day or even some random day like July thirteenth, so why St. Patrick's Day? It has me baffled."

Dax closed the trunk on his car and casually looked up and down the street, but I recognized that astute gaze. He was taking in every detail. I guess you can take the agent out of the city, but you can't take the federal agent out of the man. He asked, "Any idea how long this has been going on? Maybe that's the key, and John was supposed to be in contact with a local. How did they meet and when? I have a niggling feeling that is an important key to all of this." He leaned closer to me. "Did Gage tell you about the pot that was used to hit our victim?"

"Do you know?"

"I didn't tell you, but it was a bastible. It's a kind of kettle which coincidentally is also known as a pot a leprechaun used for their gold."

I could feel my eyes go wide. "That is very interesting, but how could someone be carting around a heavy pot without anyone seeing them?" I stood up straight. "We're going to need a reason to search the B & B. We'll find the pot somewhere on the property, but what excuse can I have to poke around?"

"Gage and the team already searched for the pot, and it wasn't there."

I gave him a sly wink. "We have skills they don't, and I bet we can find it."

His grin widened. "I do like how you think, but we have to agree that once it's found, we leave it in place and get a message to Gage first. The evidence will be critical to arrest the guilty party."

"Or parties. This might be the work of the three supposed friends."

"Why do you think it's Bailey's friends and not the local contact?"

That was a good question. "Even when I thought it was Donnie, there's no way he would have killed someone at his wife's place of business."

He grew thoughtful. "Good point." Nodding in the direction of the inn, he said, "Shall we go have a chat with Katherine and then bump into a few of her guests?"

I adjusted the strap on my shoulder bag. "You know this will be our last chance to talk to them before they take off."

"Yeah. I know."

We started to walk, and I had a few things I needed to get clear in my head. "Let's go to the bookstore first. I want to write out a few things on the clue board."

With a sweep of his arm, he said, "Lead the way. I'm here to be your backup."

Even with Gage insisting Dax be my shadow for a couple of days, I could have had a worse partner. He got the witchcraft thing and hadn't said, so far anyway, that I shouldn't be trying to solve the murder. I unlocked the door and once inside, Milo came trotting down the aisle.

"Hey, fur baby, what are you doing here?"

"Waiting for you." He jumped up to the counter next to the cash register and glanced at Dax. "I see you're finding new friends to hang out with in Nikki's absence."

"Gage thought it was a good idea." I dropped my bag and went into the small back room that served as a kitchen, storage, and the most important item in my opinion was the chalkboard that I used to work out crimes when I was at the store.

Once I carried it to the front, I pulled my phone from my bag and opened the picture of what the board at the house looked like. After I duplicated it, I stepped back.

"Two questions have been bugging me, and I know I sound like a broken record. One is the missing boot and the other is, why take the wedding dress and then ruin it by stashing it behind the tub."

Dax said, "Also, why can't Mimi locate her missing cutlery, which could be explained if a spell is being used to hide it."

Milo started to cough as if he was trying to get a hairball up. I asked, "Are you going to live?"

"It's about time you thought to look at me." He gave Dax a baleful glance. "I have some news about two of the items on your clue board."

My heart rate kicked up with the excitement of crossing two items off the list. "Which ones?"

"The boot and Mimi's utensils."

He stopped talking, and I stomped my foot. "Milo, what do you know?"

"The exact location." He began to wash his face with his paw.

Crossing my arms over my chest, I said, "Milo..." My voice held a distinct warning tone. "If you could tear yourself away from your grooming and tell me where they are, I promise a can of tuna tonight for your supper."

He paused mid-swipe of his ear. "I'm thinking smoked salmon would be delicious, with a side of sardines."

Dax smothered a laugh by covering his mouth and turned away. So much for him being my backup.

My eyes narrowed. "Do you know how much that costs per pound?"

"This information will be worth every penny. After all, Mimi's heirloom spoons are worth a small fortune by themselves."

He had a point there, but I didn't like that my familiar was basically extorting me for smoked salmon. If his information was correct and it solved two open clues, it would be worth it. "Alright, on one condition."

"Name your terms, my dear witch."

"As long as it's what we're looking for, you'll have salmon for dinner."

"Smoked, to be very precise." He was staring me down like we were at the O.K. Corral about to duel.

I nodded. "Now, where are we going?"

"Behind Tucker's Hardware store there is a small lean-to where extra lumber is stored. Go all the way to the back and there's a piece of plywood leaned up against the wall. Once you tip that forward, you'll find the boot and the box that belongs to Mimi."

I grabbed my bag and said to Dax as I rushed to the door, "Don't call Gage until we have a look first." Before he could answer me, I withdrew a pair of latex gloves from my jacket pocket. "Do you need a pair?"

He gave a low, appreciative whistle and took the gloves. "I underestimated you, Ms. Michaels."

I flashed him a grin and called over my shoulder, "Milo, lock up when you leave and see you at home."

Before he could remind me again about his dinner, I closed the door with a firm thud, and Dax and I race walked through the town green, taking the shortest route to the alleyway next to the hardware store.

"Shouldn't we let Tucker know what we're about to do?"

"Too many people will be in there this time of day. But we'll have to tell him if Milo's information is accurate."

"How do you think he found the stash?"

I shrugged. "The familiar network."

"Huh. I thought that only happened in my hometown." He chuckled, "Are you really buying Milo smoked salmon for his dinner?"

I ran down the alley as soon as we were away from anyone who might be watching. "Are you kidding? If I didn't, I'd never hear the end of it, and he wouldn't help me anymore."

"He would have to; it's part of the familiar witch connection."

As we drew closer to the opening, I slowed. "You've met Milo. Do you think he's the type of familiar to not hold a grudge?"

"I guess you're right. He is a bit snarky." Dax withdrew a small flashlight from his pocket and said, "Stay behind me."

I stepped in front of him and took his flashlight. Grinning, I said, "You stay behind me since you're supposed to have my back."

He allowed me to go first and muttered under his breath, "Gage will kill me if anything happens to you."

"Then we'll make sure that doesn't happen. Now keep

your eyes peeled." I snapped on my gloves and cautiously crept forward, sweeping the flashlight from side to side just in case there was anything else that looked suspicious. The beam illuminated the back corner, and just as Milo said, there was a sheet of plywood leaning against the wall. It was at an odd angle. As I drew closer, my heartbeat quickened. The thrill of almost uncovering an important clue was always exciting to me. And for once there wasn't a crazy person breathing down my neck as I did.

I pulled the sheet away from the wall and leaned it up against a wooden crate.

Dax said, "What do you see?"

"A box that looks like it could be the walnut flatware chest from my aunt's house and a paper bag."

"No boot?" I could hear the disappointment in his voice as he peered over my shoulder.

"My guess is it will be in the bag." I was about to go behind the plywood when Dax touched my shoulder.

"Let me. If it is evidence, it was discovered by a police officer and can be used to prosecute the guilty party." I stepped aside to allow him to go in front of me while I trained the flashlight on the bag. In my gut I knew it was the missing boot.

Dax took several pictures of the items before he carefully folded back the sides of the bag. "Hand me the flashlight, please."

He took it and tipped the bag toward him. "It's the missing boot."

I exhaled. Finally, something was going our way. "And can you open the box to make sure it's Aunt Mimi's?"

He lifted the lid from the wooden box and the cutlery glittered gold even in the dim lighting. "Jackpot. Milo can have a double helping of salmon on me."

I held up my cell. "I'll call Gage since we still need to get to the B & B. I don't want us to miss the leprechauns. But do you think while we wait for Gage, we can take a peek inside the boot and see if there's a map there?"

"I'm sure whoever took the boot must have found the map." Dax arched his brow. "But if I were to go out and see if Gage was coming..." His words trailed off and the implication was clear.

I grinned. He might be law enforcement, but he was as curious as I was, and I could bend the rules he couldn't. "I think you should go outside and wait for Gage. I'll be right out."

He gave me a knowing wink. "Glad we're on the same page." Dax handed me the flashlight. The moment he turned his back, I was already peeking inside the bag. I carefully withdrew the boot and stuck my hand down the shaft. I tugged on the liner, but there was nothing there. Disappointment flared, and I started to put the boot back into the bag when I turned it sole side up. I once had read a book where a female spy would hide things in the soles of her shoes. Could it be possible that John might have done the same thing?

I tried to lift the leather, but it was solid. Running my fingers over the edges of the heel, I felt a tiny space that shouldn't be there. It slipped to one side and there was a slip of paper. I glanced over my shoulder to make sure I was alone before I unfolded it. Carefully, I smoothed it out and took several pictures without taking the time to read it. Returning the paper and replacing the boot in the bag, I put it back in the same place where we found it.

Gage's voice boomed. "Lily, are you tampering with evidence?"

I twirled around and crossed my fingers behind my back. "I was just taking a peek at the boot."

Sharon and Mac were right behind him as he pointed to the exit. "Thank you for locating these items. I'll find you later, and we can talk. I understand you and Dax have someplace to be?"

I could see the twinkle in his eyes, but I didn't react. Pretending to act chagrined, I said, "Hi, Sharon. Hi, Mac. I was just leaving."

Chapter 17
Lily

After I exited the storage area, I gave a discreet wave at Dax for him to follow me. Once we were out of hearing range, I pulled off my gloves and said, "You'll never guess what I found."

"From the way you're grinning, I'm guessing it was good."

I withdrew my phone and before I pulled up the pictures, I made sure no one was paying attention as we crossed the grassy area on our way to the B & B. "Look for yourself."

He took the phone and enlarged the picture. "You found the treasure map to Black Sam's gold." He lifted his eyes to mine. "Where was it?"

I couldn't keep my grin in check. "It was in the heel of the boot." This felt like the first real break I had, and my confidence had soared in the last half hour. "Milo can have smoked salmon for the rest of the week. This was a great find for the good guys."

Handing the phone back to me, he said, "What's next?"

"We'll go to the B & B and bump into our three

suspects. One of them killed for this, and the only way to find out for sure is to have a friendly little chat. We also need to keep our eyes peeled for the bastible pot. Our killer probably tucked it away someplace, but with just a little bit of luck, we can wrap this case up by dinnertime."

His dark eyes grew serious. "Not that I want to curb your enthusiasm, but most cases don't come in a tidy package of one conversation and then an arrest."

"Maybe not in your line of work, but for me, once I narrow in on my suspect, I've been able to solve it, and Gage has arrested them. Today, you'll have that honor." I quirked my brow. "Any chance you have a pair of handcuffs on you?"

With a knowing smile, he said, "If we need them, I can produce them."

"Good, then let's get busy and wrap this up. I need to stop at the store for Milo."

As we hurried up the stone walkway, the front door opened, and Katherine was coming out. She had her shopping bag over one arm and gave us a warm smile. "Lily. I didn't know you and Dax were stopping by. I was just on my way to the store."

I held my expression neutral as this just presented us with a new opportunity. Everything was falling into place. "Katherine, we were hoping to talk with John's friends before they leave."

"They haven't come back from their search today, but you're welcome to wait for them." Katherine stepped away from the door, leaving it open for us to go inside. "I have carafes of coffee and tea on the side table in the lobby. Help yourselves."

I glanced at Dax, and he nodded as if this was a good idea. "Thank you, as long as you're sure?"

"Absolutely. Who knows, I might even get back before they do, and we can talk about the wonderful wedding."

"That would be nice." I gave her a smile, hoping to not make her worry that we would be in her home without her.

I lingered in the doorway as Dax walked in and Katherine headed in the direction of the market. Closing the door, I strode into the main lobby and said to Dax, "Are you thinking what I'm thinking?"

"That maybe a super sleuth and a federal agent walk into a building where there just happened to be a murder and are left alone to search for clues."

Dax being a replacement for Nikki was turning out to be okay. "Should we split up and cover more area or stay together?"

He didn't hesitate. "Stay together. We don't know who is behind all of what's happened, and if it turns out to be Donnie, he knows this building like the back of his hand."

"You have a point, and after he found me skulking around his warehouse, it wouldn't look great if he found me doing the same here."

Cocking his head, he said, "What was that all about?"

I shrugged, hoping to pass it off as if it was no big deal. "I went down to see if I could find out where Donnie was during the time when Katherine kept calling him. I thought it was odd then and after being there, I still think something is off."

"I want to hear all of this, but let's search and talk at the same time. The locator spell won't work since we don't really know what we're looking for other than the pot. We have a lot of rooms to cover before either Katherine or her guests show up."

"Good to know about the spell." Note to self: another thing I needed to learn more about, the limits of casting a spell. Nodding, we each took a side of the lobby, opening cabinets and drawers and even looking under cushions. I pointed to the sitting room. "Let's go there next."

We made short work of all the rooms downstairs including the kitchen and dining room but didn't find anything out of the ordinary.

I rested my foot on the bottom step. "Shall we take the second floor?"

"Lead the way."

I jogged up the stairs, the carpet absorbing the sound of our steps. If anyone had been in the inn, they'd be hard-pressed to say exactly where we were since we had been cautious about making any sounds.

Several of the bedroom doors were closed, and a few were open. Inwardly, I sighed. "I don't suppose opening the locks by magic would be a good idea?"

"It could be seen as tampering with evidence, and how could it be explained if we found something?"

I hated the fact that Dax was logical, but I was a law-abiding witch, and as much as I wanted to look inside the three most important rooms, I'd be satisfied with what was available to us for now. "You go left, and I'll go right?"

Dax moved down the hall and went into the first room on the left. I headed to the bridal suite and would work my way back. I stopped in front of door number ten and held out my hand like I was about to turn the knob when I withdrew it. I promised we'd do this the right way, but something was drawing me in. As if I had to go inside. Pushing that thought aside, I turned into the room where I discovered poor John Bailey.

Everything was exactly as it had been the last time I was

in here. Except the fingerprint dust was gone and the room looked pristine. Fat chance of finding a clue in here. I walked into the bathroom and pulled back the curtain, remembering the last time I had and the shock of finding a bootless leprechaun. Thankfully, this time it was empty. I got on my hands and knees to look under the tub. Maybe there was something that had been overlooked. But the area didn't even have a speck of dust.

I got up and had to wonder if this was me trying to manufacture evidence. I left that room and stopped again in front of room ten.

"Is there something I can help you with?" A deep voice brought me out of my thoughts. I looked up to discover Arthur walking toward me and Shay and Dylan standing in front of two other doors in this hallway.

"Hello. No, I just thought I heard someone talking in there." I didn't know what else to say and that was a weak excuse at best.

"We just got back so there isn't anyone in there." Arthur put his key in the lock and opened the door. "Would you like to take a look for yourself?"

A little voice in my head said I should wait for Dax, but the temptation to look around the room was inviting. "Thank you."

Arthur allowed me to enter the room first, and the three men quickly followed, leaving the door open but blocking my exit. The room was exactly how I pictured it. The bed was neatly made, a partially filled suitcase propped open on the luggage rack. In the open closet was a leprechaun suit, but I didn't see a pair of boots. I crossed the room, walking around an overstuffed chair and hassock to look out the window. I wondered what view Arthur had and noticed it was a clear line of sight to the backyard which included the shed and trash bin. Was it possible he could have thrown the boots from his room? It was something to consider. The bathroom door was open and nothing in there looked out of place either.

Brightly, I said, "Looks like it was just my imagination." As I made my way around the hassock, my shoe connected with something hard, and I tumbled forward. I cried out, "Help!" Hoping to catch myself before I hit the floor, someone grabbed my arm. I looked up, and it was Arthur. Concern was etched on his face.

"Are you hurt?"

I winced as I put pressure on my foot to take a step. "Just my toe. What have you got stashed under there?"

"Nothing." He looked to Shay and Dylan. "Did one of you put something under here?"

Before they could answer, Dax pushed them aside. "Lily, what happened?" He gave the three men a stare that could freeze water. "What's going on in here?"

Arthur held up his hands. "Nothing. I found the lady standing outside my room when we got back, and she wanted to poke around. I've got nothing to hide, so why not let her do her nosy stroll, and we can get back to packing."

Dax looked at me. "Why did you cry for help?" He took a step closer and lowered his voice. "Did one of them try to hurt you?"

"I tripped on something sticking out of the hassock." I bent over and picked up a corner of the tailored fabric exposing a round, squat black kettle. "Who does this belong to?" I took my time looking from one man to the next until I came back to Arthur. "This is your room. Should I deduce it belongs to you?"

He tipped his chin up in challenge. "Why would I have a pot in my room, hiding under a piece of furniture?"

"Very good question," Shay said.

Dylan chimed in, "It's probably been here since the last guest. Heck, Arthur doesn't even cook."

"Dax, you'd better call Gage."

He gave me a solemn nod and pointed to the men. "Don't move a muscle."

He stepped into the hall, but I knew what he was about to tell Gage, that we had most likely found the murder weapon.

Arthur's face was pale. "Lily, I swear I've never seen the pot before in my life."

I couldn't help but snort. That sounded right out of a movie or cop show when the guilty party is trying to convince people of their innocence. "Maybe we should talk about a few things before the police show up and arrest you for the murder of John Bailey. Remember, your friend?"

Arthur took a step in my direction as anger flared in his eyes, his hands clenched at his sides. "That is not my pot, and if you're trying to insinuate that we're not broken up John died, you're wrong. We've been friends for years, long before this stupid treasure became a topic of conversation. And there isn't—wasn't—a better friend. All we want is for the guilty person to be arrested and charged. Then we're going back to Boston, and after talking about everything that's happened, we're never coming back."

I looked at Shay and Dylan out of the corner of my eye, but they didn't flinch as Arthur was talking. Could it be he was telling the truth and one of them hadn't turned into a murderer over a supposed pot of gold? "Why the change of heart?"

Dylan said, "Arthur, you can fill her in."

"John was the dreamer in our group, and he believed if we came up year after year, eventually we'd find the treasure. I'm not sure why it became a St. Patrick's Day event. But a few years ago, he said a local clued him in that it could only be found the day before, during, or after St. Patty's Day. We didn't want him to make the trip alone, so this became a guys' trip. It was fun getting dressed up and following whatever clues we'd manage to cobble together during the year, but this year was different. John was different. It started after his contact sent him a slip of paper. John said it was a scavenger hunt for the actual map. That was all it took to get him even more jazzed."

"Why on earth would he think a scavenger hunt would lead to a treasure map?"

"This person's family goes back generations in Pembroke Cove," Dylan said. "John had been looking for a connection, and he found it."

"How did he meet this person?" I had a hunch it might be Donnie since the pot is in the B & B and he had full access to both the murder weapon, the victim, and the back door. Not to mention the boots.

Shay said, "Sometime between last March and now. He never told us the specifics, said it was better to just have one point of contact."

I looked at Arthur, and he didn't flinch as I asked, "Who do you think killed John?"

"If I were you, I wouldn't answer that question on the grounds that it could be considered slander or worse, you could incriminate yourself in front of two police officers." Gage stood behind Shay and Dylan, and Dax was next to him.

If only I'd asked my question two minutes earlier, I would have my answer.

Chapter 18
Gage

S tanding in Arthur's room, Lily was holding court with the three men I felt had the best motive for killing the victim. And she was questioning my suspects. I had to hand it to her. Finding the pot was a stroke of amazing luck and her laser-like focus was inspiring. But she needed to stop putting herself in danger.

Lily flashed me a frosty look, and despite the situation, I could feel a flicker of an amused smile tug the corners of my lips.

Giving me a pointed look, she said, "It was a simple question of speculation."

"And one they shouldn't answer." I turned so my back was facing Lily, and I addressed the three men. "I'd like for you to come to the police station for questioning."

Shay's face blanched, and he asked, "Are we under arrest?"

"No. But you are persons of interest, and at this point had the most to gain from the victim's death. If, in fact, there is a treasure and you had found a real map, you'd be a very rich man or men. Cutting out a fourth of the prize would give you even more."

Dylan's face darkened, and his nostrils flared. "You can't accuse us of killing him. We weren't even at the inn when he died." He bobbed his head in Lily's direction. "She's our witness. She saw us leaving and can confirm the time."

"What makes you think your friend died sometime after you left?"

"He answered us from his room." Dylan looked at Arthur. "And you went back to double-check and said he was annoyed and told us to stop checking up on him, that he'd meet us later." He jabbed a finger in Arthur's direction. "Tell him."

This was new information, and before I could respond, Lily jumped in. "I thought you all left together after knocking on his door."

Arthur's shoulders slumped. "I felt awful for going off without him. John was the leader of our merry band of seekers. It didn't feel right that he wasn't with us to follow up on the more recent clue."

"Which was?" Lily stepped closer to Arthur as if her proximity would cause him to look at her.

Shay poked him in the back. "Tell her. Otherwise, you might be sitting in a jail cell later."

"He said there was a rocky outcropping up Route 1 about an hour north of here and at low tide the entrance was exposed. Inside was supposed to be another clue. We honestly felt we were one step closer to finding the gold."

Shaking my head, I knew I had to put them in separate rooms and get them to talk. Right now, they could corroborate each other's alibi. Well, except for when Arthur went back to John's room. "You need to stop talking until we get to the station."

Dax stepped aside. "Let's take a walk. The station is just a couple buildings away."

At the bottom of the stairs, Peabody and Mac were waiting for us. Dax said, "I'll stay here with Lily if that's okay. We told Katherine we'd be here when she got back."

That was one way to keep Lily from joining me at the station. "Good idea." I gave Lily's hand a quick squeeze and dropped my voice so that she was the only one who could hear me. "Good job, but stay out of that room until we can get it processed for more evidence."

I could tell by the frown on her mouth that she wasn't happy, but I didn't have time to convince her to stay out of the investigation. Besides, history showed it was a waste of breath—not that I overly minded, she always managed to unearth vital information. "We'll talk later?"

"You know how to find me." She tugged on my hand as I moved to the front door.

"Gentlemen, can we agree to keep this low-key and walk to the station? I know it's unorthodox, but there's no sense in getting people more riled up than they already are with this case."

Arthur's chin dipped even lower. "Does that mean no handcuffs?"

"They're not necessary, are they?"

Dylan said, "No need to cuff innocent men." He pulled open the door and strode down the porch steps.

We made for an interesting group. Peabody and Mac had fallen into step beside Dylan and Shay, and Arthur walked next to me.

He was quiet for a minute before saying, "I would never have hurt John. None of us would. And as far as wanting a bigger share of the spoils, the three of us never expected to find a pot of gold. It was just about four guys getting together and acting like kids dressed up like leprechauns. We were the only family John had."

"Whose idea was it to dress in costume?"

His smile was small. "John's. He said it was part of the adventure. Like when you were a kid and played pirates and wore an eye patch and pretended to be a swashbuckler with a fake sword. Window dressing, nothing more."

The conversational approach with Arthur was working. He continued, "I remember the first time he told us about Black Sam's adventures. He came alive while retelling the stories. There was an obscure mention of Pembroke Cove. That's how we ended up here. The first time we came to town was in the summer, and it was harder to get around with all the traffic. That's when Donnie and Katherine mentioned we should come during the offseason. We came back in late October the following year, and that's when he found an old book in the study—well, it was an old hand-written journal. He scoured that book, and when he discovered the fortune could only be found around St. Patrick's Day, he was hooked. So, for the last few years we came back in March."

We walked up the steps to the police station, and Mac was holding the door for us. Arthur paused before we got to the top step. "I know you must be thinking it sounds childish, but we were having a good time and not hurting anyone." He swallowed hard. "Why did someone have to kill him over a legend?"

I pointed to the open doorway. "That's what I intend to find out."

. . .

After talking for the last two hours with Arthur, Dylan, and Shay separately, they pretty much all had the same story. And none of them knew who the local person was. I had reminded them they needed to stay in town for a few more days and although they didn't seem to have the heart to continue the search for pirate treasure, they said they would. If I had to arrest them, I would have, but my case against any of them wasn't very strong. Even with the pot in Arthur's room, anyone could have walked into the inn and put it there. Security was lax at best.

I leaned back in my office chair and glanced at the clock. It was midafternoon, and I wondered if Lily and Dax were still at the inn. I grabbed my coat from the coat rack and strode out of the station. Only one way to get a couple of answers that were bugging me and that was to talk with Katherine.

When I arrived at the inn, Donnie's truck was parked out front. That would make this conversation simpler. I pulled open the door and went in. I could hear Lily's soft laugh, and I moved quicker. If she and Dax were still here, did that mean they were tugging on a new thread?

She looked up as I rounded the corner, and a smile lit up her face. Dax and Katherine were sitting with her.

Lily asked, "Gage, did you get everything wrapped up at the station? We saw Arthur, Shay, and Dylan come back about fifteen minutes ago."

I noticed a teapot and a mouthwatering plate of tiny sandwiches and cookies. "I did. Care if I join the party?"

Katherine said, "I'll get you a cup."

"Where's Donnie?"

Her eyes widened with surprise. "At the marina, why?"

"Oh, I thought I saw his truck outside." I didn't look at Lily since it was possible Katherine wasn't telling the truth.

"Oh, that's Keith. He came over to pick up a few things from the shed out back. He said there was a tool or something they needed." She smiled. "Now, I'll get your cup. Have a seat and make yourself comfortable."

I watched as she left the room and bent closer to Lily and Dax. "Have you seen Keith?"

They both said no. I pointed to the dining room. "I'll be right back. If Katherine wonders where I am, tell her I went to wash up."

Lily started to get up, but I pointed to her chair. "You'll need to stay put this time. My alibi won't work if you come with me." I hurried from the room and picked my way through the semi-darkened dining room and out the back door that was still partially hidden by the screen. Easing open the door, I saw Keith coming out of the shed carrying a large box.

His eyes met mine, and he sneered, "Detective Erikson, are you sneaking around or on official business?"

"I might ask you the same question." I pointed to the box he was carrying. "Mind if I look inside?"

He tightened his grip on the sides of the box. "You don't need to see what's in here; it's just boat business."

"I happen to like boats. Maybe I'll discover something new." Now my interest was focused on what was inside that box. I wished I was a mind reader and could see what he wanted to hide.

He cocked his head. "Got a warrant?"

I gave him a steady stare before saying, "Do I need one?"

"I have the right to privacy, and I need to get back to work, so unless you think I've committed a crime, take it up with my boss or better still, check with Katherine. I have permission to remove this box from that shed." He kicked the door closed with his foot and stomped down the side yard before disappearing at the corner.

I had to wonder how many generations of the Hansen family lived in Pembroke Cove. Could Keith be the local contact? He was comfortable around the inn, and he'd know how to get in and out easily no matter what time of day. I opened the shed door, and withdrawing my flashlight, I took a quick look, but other than sealed cardboard boxes with labels from different part companies, I didn't see anything that looked remotely like it was related to the murder.

I hurried inside, knowing Katherine would be back with my cup. Time would tell if the conversation was illuminating or not. I eased the door on the dining room closed with barely a click and moved down the hall, trying not to make any additional sounds until I reached the lavatory door. I closed that door with a thud and did my best to make my footsteps loud.

As I went into the lobby area, Katherine looked up and held out a cup of tea for me. "Just in time."

I took the chair next to Lily and across from Katherine. Thanking her for the tea, I picked up a scone. "This is an unexpected treat."

"And for me." Katherine smiled at Lily and Dax. "I've had good company this afternoon. With all that's happened, I keep waiting for the other shoe to drop. An unsolved murder can't be good for my business."

"I'm getting close to an arrest." Lily shot me a glance with such intensity that I couldn't even look at her without betraying I was stretching the truth.

Katherine refilled Lily's cup and then Dax's. "I wish there was something I could do to help."

"Actually, I was hoping you could tell me about different families that have lived in Pembroke Cove for a long time." I bit into the scone. It was tender and moist, and it hit the spot that lunch should have filled had I not been interrupted with Lily finding the potential murder weapon.

"Any family in particular?" she asked.

"I know your family goes back several generations."

She beamed. "Five, in fact, and of course, Donnie's family is five generations. Keith and Jock, who work for him, are also many generations too. Hutch, on the other hand, is three I think; they're relative newbies. Then, of course, we have Lily's family and yours, which also have deep roots in our community, along with William from the bakery and Tucker's family. Would you like me to go on?"

I held up my cup. "If you don't mind, could I have a bit more tea?"

Lily looked at me like I had gone nuts. I'd have some explaining to do later. But I got what I needed from Katherine. Now to track down Keith's alibi for the time of the murder.

"That would indicate we're looking for someone whose family roots are entrenched in this small town," Dax said.

"Or they wanted John to believe they did." Lily gave me a pointed look. "There is no way to know for certain this local person was telling the truth when he mentioned the journal his family supposedly had about the treasure."

She had an excellent point. People skirt the truth all the time. I said, "Assuming it was the truth does help solidify the case against a few people."

Katherine's eyes widened. "You think it's someone we know?"

"Sadly, I do."

She turned to Lily and Dax before looking at me again, her face pale. "Should I be worried this person was in my inn and committed not one but two crimes?" Her hand flew to her throat, and her words were strained as she said, "Could I be his next target?"

I patted her hand, hoping to reassure her. "Katherine, if I was concerned for your safety, I would ask you and Donnie to close the B & B for a few days and keep your doors locked. However, I don't think that's necessary. Whoever this person is has been more interested in the treasure than in you."

"Do you really think so?" Her voice trembled, and I felt bad even talking about this with her in a casual setting. However, I needed the information about different families, and she had certainly narrowed things down for me. With Keith's suspicious activity earlier and driving Donnie's truck—not just recently but I suspected he was the one cruising past Lily's store earlier. Since he knew his way around the B & B, it would have been easy for him to slip in, confront John Bailey, argue, hit him with an object of convenience, and then take the boots and run.

Lily was staring at me as I ran down the logical chain of events in my head. I couldn't share them with her, at least not right now. I finished drinking my tea and set the cup down. Giving Katherine a warm smile, I said, "If you'd like, I can give Donnie a call and ask him to come home, but I do believe you have nothing to be afraid of."

She narrowed her eyes. "You have a primary suspect, don't you?"

"Katherine, I can't divulge confidential information, but I do need to get back to work." I got up from the chair.

"Dax, can you meet me back at the station in about a half hour?"

"Sure thing. I'll walk with Lily back to the bookstore. I need to pick something up, and I'll be over."

Lily stood and thrust her chin up a fraction of an inch. "I need to reopen the store, but I'll see you later?"

"Yes, let's meet at your house." I waited for Lily to say goodbye to Katherine before walking out with them. The minute the door to the B & B was closed, Lily spun around and faced me. "Who are you going to arrest?"

"Keith Hansen."

Looking me square in the eye, she said, "You're about to arrest the wrong man."

Chapter 19
Lily

The minute Dax left my bookstore to head over to the police station, I began to pace the aisles. Milo dutifully trotted along beside me, thankfully not asking a thousand questions as I mulled over the clues we had so far. My instincts were on overdrive. Keith Hansen might not be the most pleasant guy, but what did he have to gain by killing John Bailey?

"Care to share what's bothering you?" Milo blocked my turn at the end of the local author aisle.

"Gage is about to arrest Keith Hansen for the murder, and I'm sure he's got the wrong guy." I stepped over Milo and continued to pace. "Logically, it has to be Donnie." Muttering more to myself than to Milo, I said, "I need my clue board." Turning in the direction of the back room, I glanced over my shoulder. "I'm going home. Are you coming with me?"

He ran down the aisle. Leaning back on his haunches, he prepared to leap and said, "Are you kidding, smoked salmon for dinner? I'm not going to miss that." Landing in my arms, he headbutted my chin.

"We have to stop at the market." It had only been a few short hours, and I had already forgotten about his special request.

In a deep kitty grumble, he said, "I can't believe you forgot."

Scratching the top of his head, I kissed it before placing him on a chair. "Since I last saw you, I've been shopping and searching for clues at the hardware store and at the B & B. When did I have time to swing by Betty's Market? Not that I need to explain myself since you know I'm trying to solve a real crime here." I put my coat on and picked him up again.

He tapped my cheek with his soft paw. "I don't say this often. You're right. But you are getting a big package of the good stuff?"

"Yes." I'm sure that came out with a tinge of sarcasm, but I didn't care. Some days all Milo thought about was his belly.

With the front door locked, I put Milo on the passenger seat and told him I'd be right back. The fresh air on the short walk to the market would loosen the cobwebs in my brain. There had to be something I was overlooking.

The bell above the door chimed when I walked in. The store had an old-world feel as if time had stood still for the last fifty years. The store had been in Liz Wilson's family since its inception, and, in fact, her great-grandmother had been the original Betty.

"Afternoon, Lily." Liz's greeting was laced with a distinct Maine accent.

"Hello Liz. I need to pick up some smoked salmon."

Liz came out from behind the counter. She was about my mom's age, but you'd never know it by looking at her. Her face was crease free except for the deep dimples in her cheeks. I guessed spending her life working in the store protected her from the sun damage that so many of us had from hanging out on the beach or on a boat.

"I've got just what you're looking for, and it's mighty tasty." She bumped my shoulder. "Special date with a handsome detective?"

I could feel the color flush to my face. I guess my romance wasn't a secret around town, but why would it be? Small towns were where everyone knew each other. We were standing in front of a display, and I picked up a package and then grabbed another one. "No, it's for Milo. He's been really good lately, and I wanted to do something special for him."

She cocked an eyebrow and laughed softly. "After I die, I want to come back as your cat."

I wasn't sure how to respond to that statement, and I had a suspicion she was a non-magical person. There was no way I was going to spill the cauldron about why Milo was special. "What can I say, he's my little fur baby." But something Liz had said sparked an idea. As far as I could tell, we were alone in the store.

"Liz, how well do you know Keith Hansen?"

She quirked her lips to one side. "I'm friends with his mom. He's not a bad guy; he just comes off that way. The Hansen kids didn't have an easy time of it after Keith's dad passed away when he was young. He got into a lot of fights in school, and I remember his mom was always worried about him. Eventually, he seemed to settle down, and I think working for Donnie White has been good for him. From what I hear, he's a good deckhand." She took the packages from my hand, and we walked to the front of the store. "Why do you ask?"

I dug in my bag and pulled out my wallet. "I was at the

marina earlier today. I'd gone down to talk to Donnie about something, and he wasn't very pleasant."

She nodded and punched a few keys on the cash register. I handed her a twenty and waited for my change. "I'm sure he was just being protective of Donnie; those two are like brothers. They'd do anything to help the other."

"I didn't know that." I put the change in my bag and took the package of fish. "Do you think he's a violent sort of a man?"

"Not Keith. He's surly, but his bark is worse than his bite. But Donnie, on the other hand, has quite a temper. Even now I wouldn't be surprised to hear he was fighting with someone. Keith is more likely needed to calm Donnie down and not the other way around."

That added more weight to my theory that Donnie was more likely a suspect than Keith. "What about Jock and Hutch? Whose side would they take if it came to fisticuffs?"

She thought about that for a minute. "I'm not sure. At one time I would have said they both would jump into the fray, but time has mellowed them. When they come in here, they're cordial."

That made my line of questioning clear as a bucket of fish bait. I held up the package. "Milo thanks you for the salmon."

As I was going out the door, Liz called after me, "Lily, be careful."

My hand was on the doorknob, and I hoped my smile would be reassuring. "Not to worry. This was just a casual conversation between neighbors."

She shook her head and said, "There is nothing random when it comes to you asking questions that could be linked back to a crime."

"Have a great night, Liz." I closed the door behind me

and hurried to my car. I needed to look at the board and do a little cross-checking of timelines. If I was right, tying Donnie to the murder would be easy and I could wrap it up tonight. When Nikki and Steve returned from their honeymoon, I'd have an interesting story to tell them.

When I got in the car, Milo sat up from his brief nap and stretched. He winked and blinked as he looked at me. "Did you discover any new clues?"

"Why would you think I was asking questions?" I started the car and pulled away from the curb.

"Puh-leeze. I know you. Besides, you were in there longer than it takes to pick up my treat."

I held back a smile. "As a matter of fact, I discovered that Keith is all hot air with nothing to back it up. But Donnie has quite a temper and with his knowledge of treasure hunting, and if he thought there was something to this legend, and he saw the map that was in the heel of the boot..." I smacked the palm of my hand to my forehead. "With all that's been going on, I need to take a closer look at that picture of the map."

Milo tipped his head. "Are you going to finish your thought about Donnie?"

"Well, he could have met John Bailey the first time he came to town, and his family goes back several generations. There has to be a family journal that was from the White family in the library at the B & B."

I pulled into my driveway and parked in front of the garage. Once Milo and I got out, we hurried up the back steps. Me, because I wanted to check out the pictures on my phone, and he was ready for the salmon.

The house was cozy warm as we entered. Milo twined around my ankles as if that was going to get me to move faster. I picked him up and set him on a chair. "Patience, my handsome familiar." His bright-green eyes never left me as I cut up the smoked salmon and placed it next to him on the chair. "How does that look?" I took a small slice from the counter, and it melted in my mouth. It was delicious.

He cocked his head and swished his tail. "Is this all I can have?"

I couldn't help but chuckle. "Not to worry, you can have more later." Leaving him to enjoy his treat, I withdrew my clue board from the pantry closet and then hurried down the hall to my office. It was time to print the pictures of the map.

The computer hummed to life, and soon the printer was sliding out eight-by-ten glossy images. I looked at each one and went back to the kitchen. "Milo, wait until you see these."

He hopped up on the table. "Stick them on the board edges and give me some room to examine them."

I grinned, realizing over the last several months I had turned Milo into an amateur sleuth. "You did great finding Aunt Mimi's cutlery and the boot which led me to find the cast iron pot. But there is one thing bothering me. Why couldn't Aunt Mimi locate her cutlery? Was there a spell protecting it when you found it behind the hardware store?"

"No, and I'm not sure why; you'll need to ask Mimi." Turning his head from one picture to the next, he asked, "These are pictures of a journal. Look at the sloppy hand-writing. Any chance this could actually be Black Sam Bellamy's log?"

"That's what I thought too." I held up my hand so I could high-five his paw, and he shook his head.

"My dear witch. It's not quite time to celebrate, but if

these pages are authentic, they would, in fact, be a game changer."

"They're hard to read." I pulled open the junk drawer and rooted around, victoriously withdrawing a small magnifying glass. "This will help." Peering closer, I began to read out loud. "Seizing ships while letting the crew and captain go, plundering massive amounts of gold bound for what is now called the East Coast." I tapped an illustration. "This looks like it might be Cape Cod where it was reported he went to see a lady before heading north. If it was, this is his last personal journal entry."

"Maybe a crew member was the ancestor of someone from town."

I straightened up and twirled the magnifying glass in my hand. "All members of the crew were lost but maybe not." I could spin the story in so many different ways, but this wasn't getting me any closer to solving the real mystery.

As if knowing what I was thinking, Milo asked, "How does this help us?"

"It adds weight to my working theory that whoever saw this figured once they put their hands on the captain's log or a journal with more details, they'd locate the gold and be rich beyond their wildest dreams." I sank into a chair. "I need to talk this out."

Milo jumped into my lap and situated himself so that he was looking directly at me.

"If Donnie had gotten to know John on previous trips, being a treasure hunter, he would be curious. This whole bit about St. Patrick's Day was to get the guys up here so they could chase clues when there were very little out-of-towners around. It would be easier to track their movements, and I'll bet that's exactly what was going on. This has been a scheme in the making, and it wasn't a rash decision."

Milo nodded. "I like where you're going with this line of thinking. Keep talking."

"Remember John and Donnie were talking about taking his boat, *Donnie's Treasure*, out this summer which makes me think they had a real destination in mind."

"With a treasure that would be valued in the millions or more, why not just share it?"

I slide my fingers over Milo's soft gray fur. "Greed."

Milo nudged my hand to scratch under his chin. "Do you really believe Donnie intended on killing poor John Bailey?"

"If you're asking if I think it was premeditated, no. But I think the two argued at some point at the B & B, probably when Katherine was running her errands. No one would think it was odd that Donnie came back during the morning, and he confronted John about the pages, demanding to see the journal and not just pictures."

"Unless it was the other way around and John was demanding to see the journal in Donnie's possession. But where is the journal now?"

I jumped up, causing Milo to land on the floor. "I have to get back to Pembroke Cove B & B. If I'm not mistaken, that journal is hiding in plain sight on one of the library shelves. But Gage wouldn't have thought to look for it. If John had been the one to have it."

Milo bumped up against my leg. "You should call Dax before you go over there. If Donnie is around, it could be dangerous."

"I'll be fine. When we came home, I saw his truck in front of the police station. I'm sure he's trying to make sure this gets pinned on anyone other than him. Besides, Arthur, Shay, and Dylan are at the inn; I won't be there alone."

I hurriedly added a bit more salmon to his plate. "Enjoy the rest of your treat, and I'll see you later." As I closed the door, I heard Milo yowl, "Call someone, anyone, for backup."

Chapter 20
Lily

I jumped in my car and drove past the police station before parking just down the road from Pembroke Cove B & B. I slung my shoulder bag over me like it was a cross-body bag. Walking quickly down the street, not wanting to dawdle in case Donnie came back while I was poking around. Before going up the porch steps, I shot a text off to Gage and as an afterthought included Dax.

At the inn, looking for a journal. It's not Keith!!! I hit send and waited for the swish of an outgoing message before opening the door. The empty lobby was dimly lit as if it was late in the evening and not nearing dinnertime. I was sure Katherine was overseeing the final preparation for the family-style dinner she served her guests.

Should I seek her out to let her know what I was going to do or just tiptoe into the study and hope I could find the right journal? I needed to find it fast, and hopefully by then Gage would meet me here. Figuring she'd defend her husband, I chose to slip into the library undetected. I partially closed the door and inwardly groaned as it creaked, praying it was open wide enough to hear if someone was coming. For half a moment, I thought about using the locating spell, but it worked in its own time, so it was better to search the non-magical way. Besides, if I did get caught, there would be less explaining to do.

I withdrew a penlight from my bag, wanting a narrow beam of light to only illuminate the spines of the books. Starting with the bookshelf closest to the door, I ran the light over spines and around small knickknacks and other interesting items like an old belt buckle. I wasn't exactly sure how I'd know I found the right journal, but I counted on my intuition kicking in. After checking each shelf, I glanced over my shoulder and listened for footsteps before I began searching the next row. Everyone must be enjoying their dinner, and I could picture Katherine bustling between the tables, being the perfect hostess.

For a moment, I felt bad that I was invading her home, looking for evidence to prove her husband killed John Bailey. But the town would support her as she dealt with the aftermath. My breath caught when I discovered a slim, worn leather-bound book among romance novels and carefully removed it from the shelf. Easing back the cover, I noticed the date inside was written out in longhand—seventeen twenty-two. Five years after Pirate Black Sam Bellamy went down with his ship.

My heart rate ticked up as I carefully leafed through the pages, looking for anything about the gold. I slowed my scrolling as I read: *I have found the ledger from the ship that went down with Captain Bellamy and his crew. He writes of riches beyond my wildest dreams. I will secure this book and begin my search to find the elusive treasure.*

I flipped the pages back to the beginning, hoping the scribe had written their name in the book. William Reese. For a moment I froze. I was right about Donnie, and now I needed to sneak out of the study and get to the police station. Gage must see this journal before he officially arrested the wrong man. I tucked the journal in my bag and secured it. I knew it was wrong to remove the book, but it was the most expeditious way for Gage to see it.

I turned, and my heart plummeted to my stomach like a lead weight. "Katherine, how long have you been standing there?" I ran a hand over my hair, trying to steady my nerves.

"Long enough to see you trying to steal a family heirloom." She held out her hand. Her eyes were flat and devoid of emotion. "May I have the journal back?"

I placed my hand over the front of the bag and straightened my spine. "Gage needs to see this. He's about to arrest the wrong person." Stepping closer to her, I said, "You don't want Keith to go to jail for a crime he didn't commit, do you?"

Katherine closed the door. I heard a distinct click of a lock being set into place.

"You don't need to worry about anything, the town will support you." I placed a hand over my heart. "I will be here for you after."

She narrowed her eyes. "After what?"

"When Donnie is arrested for the death of John Bailey." I thought it would have been obvious, but a flicker of surprise raced across her face as she laughed softly.

"You think Donnie killed that poor sop who called himself a treasure hunter?"

I swallowed the lump lodged in my throat. "Yes, but I'm sure it was an accident, and that will come out in his testimony during the trial."

"Well, slugging someone with a cast iron pot does take muscle." Tipping her head, her smile was tinged with malice. "I can see how you jumped to that conclusion. Donnie may have a temper, but he's the nonviolent type. He's more like a Category 2 hurricane—lots of wind coming out of his mouth—and he might stomp around and go outside and split wood to get out his frustration, but he just doesn't have it in him to kill anyone."

That gleam in her eye made me reconsider who had been the real culprit. "You know I don't think I ever heard the story of how you and Donnie started dating. You being an innkeeper and him being a boat captain."

"It was a story just like so many couples. We met, and I thought he was handsome, but the real attraction was that he loved hunting for treasure. You see, when I was a young girl, I found the journal you now have in your bag, and I was hooked from the first page. I've always loved history, but when I discovered my ancestor found Bellamy's log, I couldn't get enough of the story. I must have read that book hundreds of times over the years. I had the romantic notion of becoming a pirate and finding the treasure myself." Her face glowed as she talked. "Can you imagine the discovery of a priceless treasure right in our backyard? Donnie and I would spend every spare minute we had poking around the shoreline in hopes we'd stumble across it. After a while, Donnie asked me to marry him, and I said yes. After all, I couldn't let him go running around telling others what we'd been doing."

One piece of the puzzle clicked into place—marrying for treasure not love. "Is that when he started his treasure hunting charter business?" I slipped my hand in my jacket and tapped the face of my cell. I needed Gage to hear what was happening and get over here. I could feel my heart sinking. Katherine was about to do whatever was necessary to protect her husband, no to protect herself.

"He concluded, if we could spend time looking for a treasure, other people would happily spend money to chase the dream. We took a loan against the inn for him to buy the boat, and it was a smart business move. The charter has done extremely well, and I can entice guests in taking a charter while they're staying here. A double win for us."

Knowing I needed to keep her talking, I decided to get answers to a few lingering questions. "How did the leprechaun connection come up?"

She smirked. "John Bailey handed that to me on a gold platter without even realizing it. A few years back, he was here in July and complaining about all the families on the beach. It was hard for him to poke around without nosy people asking tons of questions. Back then, his friends were coming occasionally, not every year. Donnie and I tried to spend time with him each trip; chatting over a cool beverage in the evening can be illuminating. We needed to know just how close he was to finding the treasure. And we had the luxury of time when he was in Boston to continue the search."

"I get it. Concocting a story how in a slow month he could still get around easier it would be ideal. And he took the bait—hook, line, and sinker."

A grin filled her face, but her eyes were as hard as an iron kettle. "I may have underestimated you."

Ignoring the cold finger of fear that raced down my spine, I said, "But why did Donnie feel the need to destroy Nikki's wedding and take my aunt's gold cutlery?"

"And they call you the puzzle master?" With a snort, she said, "Donnie is innocent. He doesn't have the forward thinking to pull off something like this. And over the last couple of days, Keith has unknowingly set himself up as the perfect fall guy. With his temper and driving Donnie's truck, it could be said it was a classic case of right place, wrong time. And the police will find his fingerprints on the handle of the pot. I had asked him to move it for me after I used it to hit Mr. Bailey in the head." She fluttered her eyelashes. "After all, it is *so* heavy for a woman of my age, don't you think?"

My jaw dropped and after a few seconds, I snapped it shut. Katherine had just confessed. "You killed him?"

Her mouth twisted into a grimace on one side. "Darn fool. I went to take fresh towels to his room after I got the pot from my storage cabinet in the upstairs hallway. I planned on making some old-fashioned baked beans. I knocked on his door and set the towels down on the dresser. He was getting ready to leave for a day of treasure hunting when we began chatting about what he had discovered this trip. He accused me of lying to him." She shrugged her shoulders. "And we argued."

A tear glistened in her eye as she looked at me. Was it to gain my sympathy? But the nonchalant way she shrugged gave the impression she didn't care one way or the other.

"He threatened to blackmail Donnie and expose his charter business as a fraud if I didn't help him find the treasure." With a derisive snort, she said, "He couldn't find treasure if it was sitting next to him on the deck of the boat. We got interrupted by his stupid friends knocking on his door. They were ready to leave, and he told them he'd find them later."

"And then what happened? Did you and John continue to argue?" I was surprised that she was telling me everything, and then it hit me like a ton of bricks. Katherine had no intention of me being around to share my story with anyone.

"It really was an accident, me hitting him with the pot. I

was so angry I swung. He hit the floor with a thud I'll never forget. I raced to the window and waited until I thought his friends had left. I was going to move him into the shower until I could get Donnie to come home and help me, but one of his friends came back, trying to hurry him along."

I guessed she had impersonated him, probably by muffling her voice with a towel or something.

"It was then I realized leaving him in his room was asking for trouble. I rolled his body on a blanket and dragged it down the hall into the suite. I figured I'd have at least twenty-four hours before he was found. And for the record, what they say about deadweight is fact."

I didn't need more details about how she got poor John Bailey in the tub. "Katherine." I took a step closer to her and her glare stopped me in my tracks. Instead, I asked, "What happened to Nikki's dress and the dining room and why make that mess?"

"For a smart girl, Lily, you can be dense. After I got Mr. Bailey in the suite and tidied his room. You were coming over in less than an hour, and I couldn't have you just wandering around the inn. If you had the mystery of vandalism, I thought it would buy me more time."

"You created the mess and hid the dress, but why take Aunt Mimi's box?"

She shrugged. "In the moment it seemed to fit the theme, and it was a ruse to misdirect you with the leprechaun's love of gold. His boots fell off while I was dragging him, and I wanted to get them into the garbage before you got here. I was on my way to the dumpster when I remembered John had told his friends he hid something important in them. Instead, I stashed them in the dining room until I could search them later, but that was a lie too. There was nothing in them."

I braced myself at a flick of her wrist, but there was no magic.

She continued. "I was setting the scene, adding dramatic flair. I thought you'd appreciate the gesture." She extended her hand and a harsh gleam flared in her eyes. "Now, if you don't mind returning my property, we can wrap up this little get-together and I can get back to my dinner guests."

I tapped my fingertips on the bag. "Gage will need to see this."

Katherine took one menacing step and then another, closing the gap between us. "He will never see the journal, just like you'll never see another sunrise." She slid a long thin knife off the bookshelf to the right of her, another artifact from another time. Her face softened. "I am sorry, Lily. I always enjoyed our visits, but I never thought you'd sneak in and look around, and once Keith is arrested, Donnie and I are in the clear."

She lunged as she brought the knife down, slashing the air in front of me. I leaped to the side in the nick of time.

"Katherine. Stop." My mind raced with how I could disarm her, but I hadn't read my spell book at all in the last couple of weeks. I had been too busy with all the wedding activities and right now, I was kicking myself. I glanced at the locked door and concentrated on moving the latch so it would fly open. With a flutter of my fingertips, I heard a click. Success. Hopefully, the surprise of the door opening would be enough to startle her. But she never looked as the door banged against the wall. The hallway was dark. A flicker of hope welled up in me; that was something I could change. Muttering under my breath, I said, "Lights on, lights off. The opposite of what is will be."

Katherine took another menacing step and paused next

to a cluster of candles, holding the knife above her head, ready to strike again. I wasn't sure she'd miss this time. As much as I wanted to rationalize with her about how hurting me was a bad idea, Donnie appeared in the open doorway.

"Katherine, what are you doing?"

Without so much as a glance his way, she said, "Preserving our future."

Taking a chance, I focused on the trio of fat beeswax candles. Pursing my lips, I blew a steady, intentional stream in their direction. At first, the flames wavered and then caught hold. I winced when I saw what was about to happen. As the knife fell in a downward slice, she brought her arm too close to the flames. The knife narrowly missed my face, but my arm wasn't as lucky. My sleeve fell away as the blade sliced my skin and a river of blood flowed.

Katherine acted like a raging bull despite her jacket being on fire. As she raised her hand again, I held up my hand and shouted, "I banish the knife in Katherine's hand. As so I wish, it will be."

Relief coursed through me now that the knife was gone. I grabbed a blanket and wrapped it around her to snuff out the flames. "Katherine, it's over."

Tears coursed down her cheeks. "All I wanted was to find the gold. I never meant to hurt anyone."

Donnie rushed into the room and gathered her in his arms. Holding her close, he mouthed that he was sorry. I gave him a half nod.

Footsteps thundered down the hall. Gage was frantically calling my name.

"I'm in the study."

He burst through the door with Dax close on his heels. Gage scanned the room, taking note of Donnie holding a sobbing Katherine in his arms, and his face drained of color when he saw the blood dripping from my fingertips.

Rushing to my side, he took my hand in his and examined the gash. "How bad is it?"

I glanced down and the room began to spin. "I need Aunt Mimi."

Dax had his cell phone in his hand. "On it, Lily." He tossed his scarf in Gage's direction. "Wrap her arm with that."

I took the scarf and attempted to wrap my forearm with my good hand. Gage took it from me and gently finished securing it like a pressure bandage.

"I'm okay, tend to Katherine. Her arm is burned from the candles. She confessed to killing John Bailey and intended on framing Keith." I tried to pretend that my arm was fine to ward off the pain.

"Where's the knife?" Gage dropped his voice. "If you caused it to disappear, can you bring it back?"

I pointed to the chair. "It's under there."

He dropped a kiss on the top of my forehead. "I'm relieved you're safe." He tipped my chin up and looked into my eyes. "But why did you take a chance on coming here alone?"

"I thought it was Donnie and you needed the journal to close the case. I even drove by the station to make sure he was still there." I glanced at Katherine. "It never crossed my mind I was wrong."

"If it makes you feel any better, I had come to the same conclusion about Donnie."

Gage withdrew his cell and made a few calls. "Katherine, the ambulance will be here soon, but I need to place you under arrest."

She dropped her chin to her chest to avoid looking at

anyone. Donnie said, "She'll go to the hospital first and then the police station?"

Gage said, "Yes. Her burns will be taken care of, and then she'll be charged with her crimes."

Dax knelt beside me, removed the scarf, and wrapped a clean towel around the length of my arm. I flashed him a grateful smile. He said, "Mimi and Nate are on their way," and bobbed his head in Katherine's direction. "Looks like you solved another case."

I flashed him a crooked smile. Now was not the time to be thrilled with the outcome, but I was pleased with myself despite that I almost accused the wrong person. I placed my hand on the white towel which had specks of red seeping through. "This time I'll have a reminder."

Dax whispered, "If Mimi can't get rid of the scar, I have a trick or two up my sleeve."

I cocked my head. "Why are you such a good friend to me?"

He shrugged. "There's just something about you, Lily. You're fearless and determined with a witchy heart of gold. And you've become the sister I never had and always wanted."

Gage caught my eye with an arched brow. I winked and smiled at my love and then blew him a kiss. His cheeks flushed an adorable shade of pink before directing the EMTs to Katherine.

I sighed, realizing I was a very lucky woman. In the last year, I had fallen in love with the man of my dreams, gotten engaged, and acquired a friend who had become like my brother.

Dax placed a hand on the top of the towel that covered my arm. Immediately, I felt a cooling of the wound. He asked, "After today, do you think you're going to give up solving puzzles?"

Without looking at Dax, and my eyes locked on Gage, I said, "As long as you and Gage are on the force, I'll be the puzzle master."

If you loved Leprechauns & Larceny help other readers find this book: **Please leave a review now!**
Are you ready to read more from the Lily and the gang in Pembroke?
Keep reading for a sneak peek at
Magicians & Murder
A Book Store Cozy Mystery Series
Order Now
Or
Shop at Lucinda Race

Not ready to stop reading yet? If you sign up for my newsletter at www.lucindarace.com/newsletter you will receive an excerpt for Cookies & Capers, the introduction of when Lily met Milo right away as my thank-you gift for choosing to get my newsletter.

A COZY WITCH MYSTERY

Magicians
&
Murder

A
BOOK STORE
COZY
MYSTERY

Book Seven

LUCINDA RACE

Magicians & Murder
Chapter One

Lily

I looked at my watch for the third time and decided to make a pot of coffee. Wandering into the tiny kitchen that doubled as the storage room in the back of my bookstore, I cast a quick but effective spell to start the coffee brewing. I stepped into the main room and looked out the front windows overlooking Main Street. The calendar said it was April, but today the blowing flakes of snow reminded me winter still had a firm grip on the tiny town of Pembroke Cove. And still no Nikki.

My best friend had been on her honeymoon, and I was anxious to hear all about it. I blushed as I rephrased that in my head—about the vacation part, restaurants, and what they did. In turn, I was going to fill her in on the details of the case about poor John Bailey, the treasure hunter running around town dressed as a leprechaun, and the cause of his untimely death.

I looked at Milo, my gray tabby cat and familiar, soaking up the morning sun on the wide windowsill. The smile on my face changed from friend zone to business person in the blink of an eye. Standing outside the store were two couples. The women were tall and willowy and looked like they stepped from the pages of a fashion magazine. The older gentleman had piercing blue eyes, dark hair with strands of silver, high cheekbones, and a long, thin nose. He was *stop in your tracks* handsome, and next to him was the fourth person, who also was dipped in the gorgeous gene pool. He looked similar to the tall man, but younger, with blond hair and deep brown eyes. The small bell above the front door jingled as they entered.

"Welcome to the Cozy Nook Bookshop." I swept my hand from side to side. "Browse to your heart's content, and if you're looking for something specific, be sure to let me know. We have an extensive section on local history and authors in aisle one."

"Thank you." The woman with auburn hair turned to the brunette and said, "We should start there."

I took a step closer, but my pulse ticked up. Animosity wrapped around them like a cloak, and I didn't go any farther. I wished Milo would saunter by the desk. He'd get a good read on them in half a minute or less. The older man looked me up and down.

"Do you work here?" His voice was deep and rich but cold and harsh at the same time, which made no sense to me at all. It was so conflicting.

"I'm the owner." Normally, I would introduce myself, but something told me to hold back.

"I was under the impression Mimi Michaels was the store owner," the younger man said and they all nodded.

"She sold it to me a couple of years ago." I slipped my hand into my skirt pocket, hoping to find my phone, but I remembered I left it near the cash register. Turning, I crossed the room, not caring if I appeared rude, and paused at the counter. Very few people made me nervous, but these four definitely brought in the hostility of someone I had wronged. But I had never seen them before.

Milo jumped up on the counter, and without thinking, my hand slid down his back. Just the connection calmed me. He looked up, and in a soft gravelly kitty growl, he said, "Who are they and what are they doing here?"

The brunette looked our way, her eyes fixed on Milo.

I didn't answer him. Was it a coincidence she looked over at the same time he asked his question? Could they be witches from another town and that's how they knew my aunt Mimi?

Milo bobbed his head under my hand as if trying to get some attention. "She can't understand me, but she knows you can."

I could feel my protection necklace that my aunt had given me grow warm against my skin. I turned my back to her and dropped my voice to a whisper. "Who are they?" I glanced over my shoulder and noticed the woman with auburn hair stalking over to me.

"I'm Iris Herman." She pointed to the other woman. "Standing in the historical section behind me is Celeste Jaden. The younger man with her is Clay Proctor and last, but never least, is Luca Rand."

She casually looked over the counter and saw my family's book of magic, *Practical Beginnings*, and her face morphed into a satisfied smile. "Luca. I found it."

Milo jumped on top of it, effectively covering the book with his lanky body.

"I'm sorry that book isn't for sale; it's my family's history."

Luca rushed over and extended his arms, exposing a

small moon tattoo. He started to pick up a hissing Milo, who raked his claws down Luca's arms.

His eyes narrowed. "I need to see that book."

Picturing the book in my mind, I said under my breath, "I wrap this book in protection, as I wish so it shall be."

Milo turned slightly and gave me a slow wink. He knew my spell work was getting stronger and better with each passing day. I didn't need a long incantation to make a spell work if the intention was made with strength of spirit.

Luca's eyes widened, and now his attention was focused on me. "Are you related to Mimi?"

The door opened, and Nikki was standing in the doorway. She looked at the people in my shop and then at me. "Morning. Sorry I'm a little late." She closed the door with a flick of her wrist, but it wasn't the non-magical way; she was in witch mode. Her tone was sharp as she said, "What's going on here?"

"Two witches. How interesting." Luca's gaze bored into Nikki, but she didn't flinch.

"We're the Magicians. I'm sure you've heard of our show. We're holding a single performance at the Lights Out movie theatre in town tomorrow night. You should come as our guests." He handed me two tickets that seemed to appear from thin air. When I didn't accept them, he placed the tickets on the counter very close to where my book and Milo were.

This time the low and ominous growl that came from Milo sounded more like a wild cat ten times his size, and I had never heard that from him before.

Luca withdrew his hand and gave me a smug smile as if to tell me I had won this round but not the war. In my gut, somehow, I knew more skirmishes were to come in regard to my book of magic.

"Clay. Celeste," he called over his shoulder, then inclined his head to give me a sinister smile. "Until next time, Ms. Michaels."

The other two magicians joined Iris and Luca at the counter as Nikki opened the door the way she had closed it, with a flick of her wrist. They filed out the door in a single line, and Luca was the last to leave.

"Nice parlor trick."

Nikki took one step closer to him. Her voice was colder than the wind coming off the ocean as she said, "Tricks are for wannabes."

He lifted a shoulder in a casual shrug. "I look forward to seeing you again."

Without another word, he crossed the threshold. The door slammed behind him, and the lock clicked into place. I could hear Luca chuckle as if Nikki's actions were amusing.

Rushing across the room, she was beside me, wrapping her arms around me in a tight hug. "What was that all about?"

"I'm not sure. But let's not talk about the people who left. I want to hear most of the tidbits of your honeymoon."

Her laughter filled the room, and relief washed over me as the oppressive air in the shop dissipated. She dropped her arm to her side and held up a bakery box. "I haven't fired up the oven yet, so I swung by the Sweet Spot. William had a box of cinnamon pecan buns ready and waiting for me. It was like he knew I'd be by for something sinfully delicious."

"And the coffee should be ready." Milo was still sitting on my book, and I dropped a kiss on his head. "You deserve a special treat."

He stood and stretched his back into an arch. "Smoked salmon?"

Now I laughed. "Not today, and besides, you just had some." I scratched under his chin.

He tipped his chin up so I could scratch a new spot and muttered, "That was over two weeks ago." He hopped down and padded over to the wingback chairs, which was my favorite place to enjoy a hot beverage and a pastry.

Nikki took the bakery box and set it on the small table between the chairs that had a view of the street. The idea that I could watch people in town comforted me since I didn't want the group of magicians to make a repeat visit. But once Nikki took off, I'd give Mimi a call and find out what the scoop was with these people and why they would want my book. A while back, Nikki had tried to help me with a spell, and when she looked at the pages, they were blank. From what my aunt said, only a member of the Michaels family could actually read the book.

I poured coffee into a carafe, then added a sugar bowl and creamer pitcher along with two plates, cups, forks, and napkins. The idea of calling Gage and letting him know what had happened flitted through my mind, but there really wasn't anything to tell other than rude customers wanted to purchase a book that wasn't for sale and then gave us tickets to their performance. Giving them the benefit of the doubt, I thought maybe they had been tired from their trip and that's why the sour moods.

Picking up the tray, I hesitated. I had promised Milo a treat, and he was sitting in my chair, patiently waiting.

I filled a small ball with catnip and rolled it across the floor. "Here you go."

He batted it back to me, and if a cat could cock a brow, he would have. "Tuna, please?"

I knew that snark in his tone, and it was easier to comply than not. Besides, he had protected the book from

Luca, so a can of tuna was the very least I could do. Making quick work of opening the can, I filled his bowl and put it on the chair for him. "Milo, thank you for trying to help."

"My dear witch, it's part of my responsibilities as your familiar. And I must say your protection spell has come a long way over the last few months. I could actually feel the surge the moment you cast it. Very powerful indeed."

"Sadly, that is what gave Luca the confirmation I'm a witch. I would have preferred to keep that on the down-low. Non-magicals typically can't handle it."

"Detective Cutie doesn't have an ounce of magic in his veins, despite his mother being a very powerful witch."

I wanted to chuckle at his reference to Gage. "He takes after his father, Burke. But Gage might have some magic in him."

"Glinda's magic would have shown up by now if he had inherited any." He began to eat his tuna. "You know that's the risk you run if you marry him and have kids. They could turn out to take after their father."

I set the tray down on the table and scooped Milo up from the chair, hugging him. "Would that be so bad? Heck, I didn't know I was a witch until a few months ago. It wasn't so bad not having magic."

Milo wriggled out of my arms and dropped down to the floor. "Never say that again! If you had been open to your powers, you'd be a much better witch today." He turned his back to me and waited for me to move his plate of tuna to the floor. When he continued scarfing down the fish, I could have sworn he grumbled, "Not that I didn't try."

I stepped over Milo and joined Nikki who was patiently waiting for me. "Some things haven't changed since you've been honeymooning. Milo and I are still bickering, and I may have overreacted to the situation with Luca Rand and company."

Nikki took the carafe and poured us each a mug of coffee. "That's not how I see it. That guy was not being friendly. He wanted something that you had, and if I hadn't walked in, he might have found a way to get your book. He could be a witch since he made that crack about parlor tricks."

I sniffed. "I protected it and Milo."

She gave me a side-eye. "There was extremely toxic energy when I walked in, and as soon as we're done inhaling our pecan rolls, we're going to smudge the store." Looking around, she said, "You know what, we're not waiting. Come on."

She leaped up and rushed into the back room where I stored various herbs and a few other items like candles for when I had been practicing how to light one. Nikki was on a mission, and I wasn't about to suggest that it could wait.

When she returned, she had an already smoking smudge stick, and she began walking up and down the aisles. I opened the front and back doors and with my arms wide, I tipped back my head and closed my eyes. I could picture myself sweeping out the doors the bad vibes that lingered almost unfelt, but Nikki was right. This was the best thing to do under the circumstances. A short time later we had both finished and I closed the doors by standing in the middle of the room, looking first to the front and then to the back door, willing them to close and lock.

Nikki clapped her hands. "Impressive. When did you learn that?"

"I'm not sure where it came from. I just felt that I could, and it worked." My lips twisted up one side, and I gave her a side-eye look. "Did you just do that for me?"

She held up both hands. "Most definitely not. I never mess with another witch's spell. It's rude."

Now that the shop felt like home again, I gestured to the chair. "Now, let's get down to the most important question. How was the honeymoon?"

"It was great, but you need to fill me in on how you discovered who killed John Bailey and why? And don't leave out the juicy details of how you figured it out before your fiancé."

I smiled when she mentioned Gage, my favorite police detective and the love of my life. "It was all about the treasure and an old family journal." I shook my head from side to side. "Another tragedy, and hopefully our last. The only good things that came out of it was you had a beautiful wedding and we got my aunt's cutlery back."

"I was worried it would never be found after Mimi was gracious enough to allow Steve and me to use it on our wedding day. But why was it taken?"

"Your wedding proved to be the perfect distraction to cover up the real crime."

Nikki handed me a plate with a luscious-looking pecan bun. "Until you put your puzzle skills to work and discovered who had done what."

I took the plate and smiled. "I can say I hope we never have another murder wave in Pembroke Cove again. Five people dying in the span of a few months is just so not good for tourism." I cut the bun with my fork and popped the piece in my mouth, letting the flavors dance across my tongue. "Now the next puzzle that needs to be solved is, how does William knock this recipe out of the oven every single time?"

A Free Story for You

Have you enjoyed Leprechauns & Larceny? Not ready to stop reading yet? If you sign up for my newsletter at www. lucindarace.com/newsletter you will received Cookies & Capers which is the start of Lily and Milo's adventure as my thank-you gift for choosing to get my newsletter.

Cookies & Capers

I stood in front of the old wood and glass door as I pocketed the keys to the Cozy Nook Bookshop. Aunt Mimi had signed her bookstore over to me. She said it felt like giving me her baby. But I loved the shop as much as my aunt did. We had worked together for the last twelve years. After attending the University of Maine, I had a degree in history and education. I had always wanted to be a teacher, but jobs were scarce and after substituting for a few years, I moved back to my hometown of Pembroke, Maine, and Aunt Mimi hired me as soon as I unpacked my suitcase.

Spending time with my aunt, learning the business, had been the best experience. I offered to buy the shop when she wanted to retire, but she wouldn't hear of it. As long as she had free books for life, and her long-term boyfriend Nate, she said it was a fair deal. From my point of view, I had built-in backup for years to come.

Now that I was the bookshop owner, Aunt Mimi was no longer coming in every day which meant her cat, Phoenix, wasn't either and the space felt empty without a kitty lying in the window or skulking about as kitties do. I was off to the Pembroke Animal Palace to see if I could find a match.

It was a short walk in the bright noonday sun. The spring air from the ocean carried a tang of salt, but the breeze was refreshing. I waved to one of my best friends, Gage Erikson, as he drove past in his police-issued sedan. My heart fluttered in my chest.

He was a detective on the force. Not that we had much crime in our small seaside town. But one of these days I was going to get brave and tell him I had been carrying a torch for him since we were in ninth grade. What's the worst thing that could happen? We'd still be best friends, right?

I continued down the brick sidewalk, waving to William North from the Sweet Spot Bakery. He was sweeping the area around the small bistro tables in front of the bakery. William was wearing a large pristine white apron and a wide smile. A deep inhale confirmed my suspicion. He was baking cookies. My mouth watered. I did a half turn and went back to where he was finishing up. "Good morning, William." I bobbed my head in the shop's direction. "What is that tantalizing smell?"

He held open the brightly polished glass door. "One of your favorites, Lily. Chocolate chip and pecan cookies. Can I interest you in one before you continue on your mission?"

I gave him a side-look. "Mission?"

He chuckled. "Over the years my Lulu had said you

had two speeds, strolling and purposeful. Just now it was purposeful so hence you're on a mission."

"I'm going to the shelter, hoping to find a kitty. The shop is lonely now that Phoenix is home every day with Aunt Mimi, and I think a cat napping in the window adds an air of serenity to the place."

"Unless you're allergic."

He had a point, but I was not willing to be deterred. I smiled. "I'm always happy to deliver to a customer." I leaned over the glass bakery case, like a kid pressing her nose against the candy case. "You made sugar cookies too and frosted them?" I sighed. I was going to need to exercise more if he continued to bake all my favorites. He was smiling at me as I looked up. "Are the chocolate pecan ready?"

He wiggled his eyebrows. "I have a tray cooling in the back."

"Then can I have one of those and a sugar cookie, but to go?"

With a flick of his wrist, he snapped open a white bakery bag and called over his shoulder. "Jerilyn, would you please bring out the last batch of cookies?"

I heard a muffled, coming, and smiled. "It's good that Jerilyn stayed on." I said nothing about his beloved wife Lulu. Rumor had it she was ill and not doing well.

He nodded. "It is. She's a hard worker and excellent with the customers."

Jerilyn bustled in from the back room carrying a large stainless-steel tray. It was lined with parchment paper and cookies the size of the palm of my hand. It was going to taste so good with a hot cup of tea later.

William put two in the bag, along with two sugar cookies, and then he handed it to me. I paid for my cookies and thanked him. "Stop by the shop later. You might just get to meet my new fur baby."

"Sounds like a plan." He grinned and crossed his arms over his rounded midsection. "You're more like your aunt than you realize. Ever since she opened that bookshop, she's had a cat, too."

I paused, tucked the bakery bag in my tote, and with my hand on the door, I turned and gave him a wide grin. "And now it's time I carry on the tradition." With a jaunty wave, I called, "Wish me luck."

Cookies & Capers is only available by signing up for my newsletter – sign up for it here at www.lucindarace.com/newsletter

Love to read?

Cowboys of River Junction

<u>Stars Over Montana</u>
*The cowboy broke her heart but he never stopped loving her.
Now she's back ready to run her grandfather's ranch...*

Hiding in Montana
Can love flourish while danger lurks in the shadow?

Moonlight Over Montana
*Will a single mom find love with the handsome cowboy who
saved her and her daughter from danger?*

Second Chances in Montana
*Twenty years later Renee and Hank are back where they fell
in love but reality is like a spring frost and is a long-distance
relationship their only option for their second chance?*

The Sandy Bay Series
<u>Sundaes on Sunday</u>

Love to read?

A widowed school teacher and the airline pilot whose little girl is determined to bring her daddy and the lady from the ice cream shop together for a second chance at love.

Last Man Standing/Always a Bridesmaid
Barrett
Has the last man standing finally met his match?

Marie
Career focused city girl discovers small town charm can lead to love.

Price Family Series
Breathe
Her dream come true may be the end of his...
Crush
The first time they met was fleeting, the second time restarted her heart.
Blush
He's always loved her, but he left. Now he's back...the question, does she still love him?
Vintage
He's an unexpected distraction, she gets his engine running...
Bouquet
Sweet second chances for a widow and the handsome billionaire...

Holiday Romance
The Sugar Plum Inn
The chef and the restaurant critic are about to come face to face.

Last Chance Beach
Shamrocks are a Girl's Best Friend

Love to read?

Will a bit of Irish luck and a matchmaking uncle give Kelly and Tric a chance to find love?

A Dickens Holiday Romance
Holiday Heart Wishes
Heartfelt wishes and holiday kisses...

Holly Berries and Hockey Pucks
Hockey, holidays, and a slap shot to the heart.

Christmas in July
She's the hometown girl with the hometown advantage. Right?

A Secret Santa Christmas
Christmas isn't Holly's thing, but will a family secret help her find the true meaning of Christmas?

It's Just Coffee Series 2020
The Matchmaker and The Marine
She vowed never to love again. His career in the Marines crushed his ability to love. Can undeniable chemistry and a leap of faith overcome their past?

The MacLellan Sisters Trilogy
Old and New
An enchanted heirloom wedding dress and a letter change three sisters lives forever as they fulfill their grandmothers last request try on the dress.
Borrowed
He's just a borrowed boyfriend. He might also be her true love.

Love to read?

Blue
Will an enchanted wedding dress work its magic one more time?

McKenna Family Series
Between Here and Heaven
Ten years of heaven on earth dissolved in an instant for Cari McKenna when her husband Ben died.
Lost and Found
Love never ends... A widow who talks to her late husband and her handsome single neighbor who has secretly loved her for years.
The Journey Home
Where do you go to heal your heart? You make the journey home...
The Last First Kiss
When life handed Kate lemons, she baked.
Ready to Soar
Kate will fight for love, won't she?
Love in the Looking Glass
Will Ellie's first love be her last or will she become a ghost like her father?
Magic in the Rain
Dani's plan of hiding in plain sight may not have been the best idea.

Cozy Mystery Books
A Bookstore Cozy Mystery Series 2023
Welcome to Pembroke Cove, where witches and murders are multiplying...
Books & Bribes
It was an ordinary day until the book of Practical Magic

Love to read?

conked Lily on the head causing her to see stars. And then she discovered her cat, Milo, could talk.

Catnap & Crimes
A witch, a snarky familiar and murder...

Tea & Trouble
When reading tea leaves turns to murder can Lily solve this latest case?

Scares & Dares
What does a haunted house and murder have in common? New witch Lily Michaels is determined to solve the case.

Holidays & Homicide
Even a fun event like the annual Glow & Glide can lose its charm when a body is discovered on the ice.

Leprechauns & Larceny
A leprechaun, a wedding, and pirate treasure, Oh My!

Magicians & Murder Spring 2024
When four magicians roll into town for a show more than fun is on one person's mind.

Artifacts & Amulets Summer 2024
Milo has been keeping secrets, which can be deadly.

Cranberries & Criminals November 2024

Social Media

Follow Me on Social Media

Like my Facebook page
Join Lucinda's Heart Racer's Reader Group on Facebook
Twitter @lucindarace
Instagram @lucindraceauthor
BookBub
Goodreads
Pinterest

About the Author

Award-winning and best-selling author Lucinda Race is a lifelong fan of reading. As a young girl, she spent hours reading novels and getting lost in the fun and hope they represent. While her friends dreamed of becoming doctors and engineers, her dreams were to become a writer—a novelist.

As life twisted and turned, she found herself writing nonfiction but longed to turn to her true passion. After developing the storyline for A McKenna Family Romance, it was time to start living her dream. Her fingers practically fly over computer keys as she weaves stories of mystery and romance.

Lucinda lives with her two little dogs, a miniature long hair dachshund and a shih tzu mix rescue, in the rolling hills of western Massachusetts. When she's not at her day job, she's immersed in her fictional worlds. And if she's not writing romance or cozy mystery novels, she's reading everything she can get her hands on.

Printed in the USA
CPSIA information can be obtained
at www.ICGtesting.com
LVHW010748310324
775971LV00039B/1467